Kristy Power!

Other books by
Ann M. Martin

P.S. Longer Letter Later
(written with Paula Danziger)
Leo the Magnificat
Rachel Parker, Kindergarten Show-off
Eleven Kids, One Summer
Ma and Pa Dracula
Yours Turly, Shirley
Ten Kids, No Pets
Slam Book
Just a Summer Romance
Missing Since Monday
With You and Without You
Me and Katie (the Pest)
Stage Fright
Inside Out
Bummer Summer

THE KIDS IN MS. COLMAN'S CLASS series
BABY-SITTERS LITTLE SISTER series
THE BABY-SITTERS CLUB mysteries
THE BABY-SITTERS CLUB series
CALIFORNIA DIARIES series

Friends Baby-sitters Club Forever

Kristy Power!

Ann M. Martin

AN
APPLE
PAPERBACK

SCHOLASTIC INC.

New York   Toronto   London   Auckland   Sydney
Mexico City   New Delhi   Hong Kong

*The author gratefully acknowledges
Ellen Miles
for her help in
preparing this manuscript.*

ISBN 0-590-52332-5

12 11 10 9 8 7 6 5 4 3 2 1   9/9 0 1 2 3 4/0

Printed in the U.S.A.   40

First Scholastic printing, November 1999

❁ Chapter 1

Batman vs. The Joker.

Superman vs. Lex Luthor.

Men in Black vs. huge, ugly alien bugs.

Kristy Thomas vs. Cary Retlin.

Yup, it's like that.

What do they call them in the comics? Archenemies? Well, that's what Cary and I are. We have been ever since he moved here.

Where's "here"? Good question. Obviously I haven't filled you in on all the details. "Here" is Stoneybrook, Connecticut, my hometown. I've lived here all my life, which is approximately thirteen years. My name, in case you haven't guessed, is Kristy Thomas. Kristin Amanda Thomas, if you want to be formal.

Or irritating. Cary used to call me Kristin all the time, just to try to get my goat.

Why he would want my goat, I don't know. I don't even *have* a goat, to tell you the truth. I have a humongous puppy named Shannon and a wacky little kitten named Pumpkin. Plus various goldfish and a pet rat, all of whom actually belong to my younger siblings and stepsiblings.

I guess I'd better give you the rundown on my family now. First off, there's me. I'm short, with brown hair and eyes and a distaste for dressing up. For me, "dressing up" = wearing anything fancier than T-shirts and jeans. I love sports, especially softball, which I play (I'm on the school team) and coach (Kristy's Krushers, a team of little kids in Stoneybrook). I'm energetic, opinionated, outspoken, and full of great ideas. (I'm not as conceited as that may sound. It's just the truth.) My best idea ever was for the Baby-sitter Club, or BSC, a club that's more like a business. It's a bunch of baby-sitters, who also happen to be good friends, who work together to provide quality sitting for a lot of regular clients.

Then there are my three brothers. Two of them are older than me (Sam's fifteen, and Charlie is seventeen). David Michael is younger (he's seven). I'm very close to all three of them, and to my mom.

Why? Well, partly because we had to pull together as a family years ago when our dad walked out on us.

Believe me, that hurt. A lot. It hurt back then, and it still hurts now. I didn't have much contact with my dad for years, except for the occasional birthday card. Recently, though, he seems to be interested in coming back into our lives. Maybe. I think. It's too soon to tell, really. He decided to remarry not long ago, and he invited me and my older brothers to the wedding. I like his new wife, Zoey, a lot. As for Dad — well, as I said, it's too soon to tell.

Meanwhile, back in Stoneybrook, life has gone on without him all these years. We struggled along, just the five of us, for quite awhile. Then this great thing happened: My mom, who deserves the best, met a fantastic guy.

To be honest, I didn't think he was all that fantastic at first. But he's grown on me. A lot. Now I'm crazy about him, which is a good thing, because my mom married him and we moved across town to live in his mansion.

Yes, you heard me right. My stepfather, Watson Brewer, lives in a mansion. That's because he's a real, live millionaire. As in, bucks galore. Not that he acts rich or anything. In fact, if you didn't know Watson was rich you wouldn't be able to tell by the way he acts. He's never stuck-up or rude. And he dresses like a normal person. I used to picture millionaires in top hats and tails. Now I know they wear sweatsuits.

So. My mom married Watson, and we went to live with him. I gained two stepsiblings in the deal. Karen's seven and Andrew is four, and they live with us part-time. I love them a ton.

I also gained another sister, Emily Michelle. She's a toddler, a Vietnamese orphan adopted by my mom and Watson. Adorable? You bet. You've never seen anything cuter.

All of us fit comfortably into that mansion, along with Nannie, my grandmother. She came to live with us after Emily Michelle arrived. Nannie's not a sit-and-knit grandma. She's a busy, active woman who loves to watch MTV and who drives around in a car the color of bubble gum.

Now, where was I? Oh, right. Cary Retlin. My archenemy.

I was thinking about Cary on this gray December day because I happened to be sitting behind him in English class.

I was staring at the back of Cary's head, which is covered in straight, longish dirty-blond hair, and I was wondering what makes him tick. I've never figured Cary out. I'm not sure I want to either. But if I did, it wouldn't be easy. He's an enigma. Good word, huh? It means, according to my dictionary, "one that is puzzling, ambiguous, or inexplicable." That's Cary, all right.

Cary is relatively new in Stoneybrook, but he's certainly made his mark. Especially at SMS, or Stoneybrook Middle School, where I'm in the eighth grade. Any time there's mischief happening at our school, you can bet Cary's involved. At one time he was even part of a prank-pulling group called the Mischief Knights. At least I think he was. You can never be sure of anything in Cary's case.

He's sure of himself, though. No question about it, Cary has a pretty good opinion of Cary. You can see it in the way he swaggers through the halls, in the way he lifts one eyebrow when he's talking to you, in the way he smirks his little smirk. Cary is an arrogant, smart-alecky kind of guy. He's obnoxious, but not in an Alan-Grayish sort of way. (Alan Gray, another boy in our grade, is obnoxious in an immature, spitball-throwing way.)

And yet I don't hate Cary. Not exactly. I just, well, I wish I could get to him the way he can get to me.

For some reason, when Cary first moved here he targeted me and my friends in the BSC. He has given us a hard time in more ways than I can count. Why? Because, he says, "complications make life more interesting." Excuse me, when did I ever say I was bored?

To be honest, he *has* kept us guessing. And I hate to admit it, but sometimes his tricks have been . . . well, not boring. Like the time he challenged the members of the BSC to a mystery war and planted clues all over the school for us to find and figure out. Annoying? Yes. A big yawn? No.

Anyway, there I was, staring at the back of Cary Retlin's head. Then Mr. Morley — Ted — interrupted my thoughts.

"Who can tell me what makes a good biography?"

He stood in the front of the room, smiling at us. In one hand he held a copy of *A Life of Discovery*, a book about Eleanor Roosevelt that we had read in class at the beginning of the semester.

Ted is a terrific teacher. I think he's my favorite this year. And I've only had him for a month!

You may be wondering why I call him Ted. It's because he told me to. Well, not just me. He told the whole class to call him that. "It's my name," he said, shrugging. "When I hear 'Mr. Morley' I think people are talking about my dad."

It's not always easy to remember to call him Ted, but we try. When we forget, he just smiles. Then we remember.

Ted is young for a teacher. He's probably twenty-five or something. He's a big guy with black hair and a big black beard. Big hands, big feet, and a big old stomach. He's kind of like a teddy bear, in fact.

Why has he been our teacher for only a month? He took the place of our regular English teacher, Mrs. Simon, when she had her baby. That wasn't supposed to happen until the middle of January, but the baby had other plans. I guess he wanted to be here for Christmas. Anyway, the baby's fine, but Mrs. Simon started her maternity leave early, so we ended up with Ted ahead of schedule.

Ted is the best. Everybody loves him. He's not like a regular teacher at all. He runs the class without *running* it, if you know what I mean. He's definitely in charge, but he doesn't act as if he's smarter or better than his students. He listens to what we have to say, really *listens*.

He was listening now as kids in the class spoke up about biographies. "I think it's good when the writer lets you get to know the person in a new way," said Austin Bentley. "Showing you what Martin Luther King was like as a little kid, or something like that."

"Good," said Ted. "Anybody else?"

"It should be fun to read," volunteered Cokie Mason, who is one of my *not* favorite people in the world. "Almost like a soap opera."

Ted nodded. "Sure," he said. "A biography is a story, after all."

This boy named Jeremy spoke up. "But not everybody's life is all that interesting," he said. "So a good biography should also be about a special person."

Ted considered that. "I'm not sure I agree with you there, Jeremy. I happen to think everybody's life *is* interesting. Which leads me to your next assignment."

We groaned. Not because we hate the assignments Ted gives us. Actually, he usually assigns projects and homework that seem more like fun than schoolwork. But face it. In middle school, when a teacher mentions work, everybody groans. It's practically a tradition.

Ted just smiled. "Our next unit is called Fact and Fiction," he said. "Over the next few weeks, you'll each complete two projects. Your grade will reflect how well you complete them."

Cokie raised her hand.

"Yes?" Ted asked.

"What are the projects, and what percentage of the grade will each of them count for?"

Ted smiled again, though this time he tried to hide it. "I was just about to tell you that," he said. "The two projects, each of which will count for half of your grade, are a biography project and a fiction-reading project." He held up a hand and ticked off fingers as he spoke.

Just then the bell rang.

"Oops, time's up," said Ted. "I'll give you the details tomorrow."

Cokie looked disappointed. She'd had her pen out, ready to write down the assignments. Slowly she put it away and closed her notebook.

I was a little disappointed myself. It's funny, I've never been a huge fan of English class. But having Ted for a teacher was changing my mind. These days, English was fun. Even if I did have to spend every class period staring at the back of Lex Luthor's — I mean, Cary's — head.

❀ Chapter 2

"Take one and pass the rest back." Ted handed a stack of papers to the first person in each row.

It was the next day, Friday. I was in English class, staring once again at Cary Retlin's cowlick. Just as I was wondering why they call it a "cowlick," he turned and handed me the stack of papers. He smirked at me and raised an eyebrow. "Spacing, Kristy?" he asked.

I frowned. "No," I said, wishing I could think of a snappy retort. I took one of the papers and turned to pass the rest to Rachel, the girl behind me. Rachel used to live in Stoneybrook, then she moved to London for awhile, but now she's back. Oh, goody. Rachel has never been a favorite of mine. Still, I gave her a smile along with the stack. She smiled back. I don't think we'll become friends, but I know she and my friend Stacey McGill are getting to know each other.

I glanced at the paper and saw that it was a list of books. Some titles were familiar, such as *The Catcher in the Rye* and *A Separate Peace*. But there were also a few books I'd never heard of. It was nice to see a few unfamiliar titles; this list looked a little more interesting than our usual reading lists.

"As you can see, this is a list of books," said Ted. "Can anyone tell me what they all have in common?"

"They all have titles!" Alan Gray yelled out.

Ted smiled. "Very observant, Alan," he said drily. "Anybody else?"

"Um, they're all about kids?" asked Jeremy.

"Good thought," said Ted, looking down to scan the list. "I can see why you would say that. But it's not entirely true. Anyway, I had something else in mind."

Jeremy blushed a little, and I saw Claudia shoot him a sympathetic look.

Like Rachel, Jeremy is new at SMS. He moved here from Olympia, Washington, which sounds like a cool place to live. He's majorly cute. In fact, he's so cute that not one but *two* of my friends have had crushes on him. One is Claudia Kishi, the only full-time member of the BSC who's in my English class. The other is her one-time best friend, Stacey McGill, the one who's friendly with Rachel. Stacey and Jeremy are an item now, and Claudia and he are just friends. As for Stacey and Claudia, well, Jeremy is the reason I said Stacey is Claudia's *one-time* best friend.

Jeremy smiled back at Claudia and shrugged as if to say, *Thanks, but I'm fine.*

"I think I know," said Logan Bruno, waving his hand in the air. Logan is great. He and my best friend, Mary Anne Spier, went out for ages. They recently broke up, not long after Mary Anne's house burned down. (A major tragedy for her and her family, but at least nobody was hurt.) Logan and Mary Anne are still awkward about the breakup. No wonder. They were boyfriend and girlfriend for so long that it's hard to think of them as "just friends."

"They're all fiction," Logan said when Ted called on him. "There aren't any biographies or true stories on this list."

"Excellent," Ted said, nodding. "That's just what I was looking for. Logan, you must have remembered what I said yesterday about our upcoming projects." Ted waved a list. "This list includes works of fiction only. Some are classics, some may be destined for greatness, and some are just plain fun to read. I don't expect every one of you to like every one of these books. But I think if you look over the list carefully, you'll find that there's something for everyone."

"Even for people who hate to read?" asked a boy named Dave.

"Maybe something on this list will change your mind about that," said Ted. "That would be my hope, anyway."

Cokie held up her hand. "How many books do we have to read?" she asked.

"Just one," said Ted.

"Cool," Dave muttered.

"But I want you to read that one book really, really well," Ted added, looking straight at Dave.

"Are we going to have to write book reports?" asked Claudia.

I could hear a little nervousness in her voice. Claudia is not fond of writing. She doesn't spell very well, and she has a hard time remembering the rules of punctuation. Don't misunderstand — Claudia's very bright. She's just not crazy about school. She'd rather express herself through art than through words.

"Yup," said Ted, folding his arms.

I saw Claudia grimace.

"But I'm not looking for typical book reports where you tell the whole plot, blah, blah, blah," Ted continued. "For this book report, I want you to tell me what the book *meant* to you. How it affected you. Did it make you cry? Change an opinion? Teach you something?" Ted was looking around the room, making eye contact with each of us. "The best fiction *does* have an impact on the reader. We become the people we are partly through what we read. I want to hear how a book added to your life."

"What if we just think it's boring?" Dave asked.

"Then try another book. And keep trying, until you find one that means something to you. If nothing on the list grabs you, talk to me. I'll offer some other suggestions. I'm sure we can find one book you'll like."

Dave grumbled a little under his breath. Ted just ignored him. "In case you haven't figured it out, my mission here is to make you care about reading," he said, smiling.

Cary raised his hand. (I should mention that he manages to make that motion look cool instead of geeky.) "Okay," he said when Ted called on him, "so that's our fiction project. What about the biography thing?"

"Glad you asked," Ted answered. "I think you'll all enjoy this one. What I want each of you to do is write a biography."

I heard groans. "Of Madame Curie or something?" Rachel asked. She sounded deathly bored.

"Nope," said Ted. "It'll be about someone much closer to you. In fact, it will be a biography of someone in your class."

More groans. "But everybody in this class is a bore," said Alan. "Nobody in here is an astronaut or a rock star."

"Especially you," Dave said to him.

"But that's the point," said Ted, ignoring Dave. "I want you to figure out how to create a fascinating biography of one of your fellow students. As I said yesterday, it's my belief that everyone's life is interesting. We all have our own stories, but we rarely have the chance to share them."

"I know Cokie's story," said Alan. "Born under a rock. Raised by emus. Destined for mediocrity."

Cokie shot him a Look.

Ted raised both hands. "Enough," he said. "Let's be serious here for a minute. Does everyone understand the assignment? What I want you to do is learn the biographer's craft. It's not as easy as you might think. It involves not only interviewing your subject but using other sources. You'll talk to their friends and family, check published sources such as the school newspaper or the yearbook, and follow up any interesting leads you find. I want you to present the whole person in this biography."

This was beginning to sound like fun. Being a biographer, I realized, was not too different from being a detective. And I'm a pretty good detective, if I do say so myself. My friends and I have solved a few very interesting cases.

"Mr. Mor — I mean, Ted?" Rachel had raised her hand. "How do we decide who we're going to write about?"

"Aha, good question," said Ted. "You don't. I do. In fact, I already have. Right now I'm going to pass back a sheet that gives all the details of this project, including pairings of biographers and subjects. I pulled names out of a hat last night, so it's totally random. You and your biography partner will each write about the other. You're going to get to know each other very, very well."

I thought I heard a smile in his voice, but when I

glanced at Ted his face was serious. Then I looked down at the paper that had landed on my desk, courtesy of Cary.

Mr. Morley's "random" method had created some interesting pairs.

Alan Gray and Cokie Mason. (Now Alan would have a chance to interview those emus.)

Claudia and Jeremy. (Hmm . . .)

Logan and Rachel. (It still seemed weird to hear Logan's name paired with any besides Mary Anne's.)

Me and —

Oh, no! I stared down at the paper in shock. In front of me, I heard Cary groan.

Was this some kind of sick joke on Mr. Morley's part? Or just a cosmic blunder? Whatever it was, it was a massive mistake. I couldn't possibly work closely with —

Cary.

The one person I had no interest in learning about. In fact, I had *negative* interest in finding out anything about Cary Retlin's life. Nor did I want him learning anything about mine.

Cary turned to look at me, and for once he wasn't smirking. He looked as shocked as I felt. "This can't be," he said.

I shook my head. "No, it can't."

I thought of the last time Cary and I had worked together, during a disastrous student-teaching episode. We'd cotaught a gym class, and we'd come very close to creating mayhem on a scale that would have gone down in SMS history.

Just then, the bell rang. Everybody grabbed their stuff and headed out — everybody but Cary and me, that is. We approached Ted's desk. He was busily straightening up a pile of papers, preparing for his next class.

Cary cleared his throat. "Uh, Ted?" he began.

Ted looked up. "Yes?"

I jumped in. "There is no way — "

Cary glared at me. "Absolutely no way — "

"In a million years," I went on, "that the two of us — "

"We can't possibly — "

"There must be some mistake," I finished lamely.

"There isn't," Ted said firmly. "No mistake at all. You will be writing each other's biographies. Any other questions?"

Cary and I gaped at each other.

"In that case, I'll have to excuse myself," said

Ted. "I have another class arriving in two minutes." He smiled at us and went back to his papers.

I could have sworn I saw something mischievous in that smile.

Cary closed his mouth and I closed mine. Then we marched out of the room without speaking another word.

❋ Chapter 3

I was still in shock when I arrived at Claudia's house for our BSC meeting later that afternoon. But even in that condition, I couldn't help noticing an odd silence when I walked into Claud's room. Mary Anne wasn't there yet, but Stacey was.

In the old days (before Jeremy, that is), if you put Claudia and Stacey in a room together they'd start gabbing like mad about some sale at the mall or their parents or something. But that day I didn't hear a peep as I entered the room. Stacey was sitting at one end of the bed, leafing through the latest issue of *Teenzine*, and twirling a lock of her curly blonde hair. Claudia was sitting at her desk, stringing beads onto a leather thong.

"Kristy!" Claudia cried when I walked in. I

thought I could hear relief in her voice. Was it that hard for her to be alone in a room with Stacey?

Stacey smiled. "What's up?" she asked. Her smile was for me only. I could tell that she was carefully avoiding eye contact with Claudia.

Ugh. It's no fun having two friends who are fighting with each other. And over what? A boy. Now, Jeremy's pretty cute, but still. He's just a boy. Is any boy worth losing your best friend over?

Mary Anne arrived just as I was settling in the director's chair by Claudia's desk. She glanced around the room, and I could tell she was taking in the situation. Our eyes met and she gave me the tiniest smile. I knew she felt the way I did about the rift between Stacey and Claudia.

"Well," I said as Claudia's digital clock clicked over to five-thirty, "I guess I hereby call this meeting to order."

As if on cue, the phone rang. Claudia answered it. "Baby-sitters Club," she said. "Can I help you?" She listened for a few seconds. "Sure, Mrs. Newton. We'll call you right back, okay?" She put down the phone.

Mary Anne reached for the club record book, where she keeps track of our schedules. "What day?" she asked.

"Next Friday night. She needs a sitter while she and Mr. Newton go to a play in the city."

Mary Anne ran her finger along the page she'd turned to. "Stacey and I are free."

"Um," said Stacey, glancing at Claudia, "I'm not actually free. I — I have plans."

We all knew what that meant. Stacey had a date with Jeremy, but she didn't want to make a big deal about it in front of Claudia. Even though they weren't best buds anymore, they were making an effort to be civil to each other.

I snuck a glance at Claud. She was concentrating on her bead-stringing, pretending not to listen.

"Well, okay," said Mary Anne. "No problem. I'll be glad to take the job. I haven't spent time with Jamie and Lucy in ages." She wrote her name in the book.

Claudia called Mrs. Newton back to let her know Mary Anne would be the sitter. After she hung up, there was an awkward silence in the room.

"So — " I said.

"I heard about — " Stacey started speaking at the same time.

"What?" I asked. "Go ahead."

"No, you."

I sighed. "I was just about to say that Claudia and I had a cool English class today."

"That's what *I* was going to mention," said Stacey. "I heard that Ted gave your class an interesting assignment."

From the way she was speaking, I knew she'd heard it from Jeremy. And I was sure Claudia knew that too. So Stacey probably already knew that Claudia and Jeremy were partners. And she probably wasn't happy about it. Stacey doesn't seem too comfortable with the fact that Claudia and Jeremy get along really well. I decided to ignore that issue and bring up my own problem. "Did you hear who my partner is?" I asked.

"For what?" asked Mary Anne.

I realized she didn't know anything about the biography project, so I backed up and explained it. She nodded, looking thoughtful.

"Anyway, guess who I'm stuck with? Mr. Eyebrow. Cary Retlin."

Everybody groaned. For a moment it felt like old times, when we were all on the same side.

As usual, Mary Anne tried to be positive. You can always count on her to be sensitive and understanding. "Maybe it will be interesting," she said. "I mean, aren't you curious about what makes Cary tick?"

"I couldn't care less," I insisted, even though I'd been wondering the same thing only the day before. "And I certainly don't want him probing my most innermost thoughts and dreams."

"I won't tell him anything if he interviews me," Claudia promised. "Except maybe that story about when you threw up on the first day of school in second grade."

I grabbed a pillow and threw it at her.

"Who's your partner, Claudia?" Mary Anne asked innocently.

Claudia stopped laughing. She mumbled a name.

"Who?" Mary Anne asked.

"Jeremy," said Claudia, a little bit louder. She avoided Stacey's eyes.

"Oh," said Mary Anne, with a glance at Stacey.

The room fell silent again.

I crossed my fingers and wished as hard as I could for the phone to ring. We needed a distraction.

Silence.

Suddenly, I remembered something. "Hey!" I said. "Guess what? Last night my mom and Watson agreed to let me throw a Christmas party. You know, a real party, with decorations and food and games and dancing and everything." I was excited. I've had plenty of parties, but most of them have been pretty basic. A couple of pizzas, a video or three, and a bedroom crammed with girls in sleeping bags. This party was going to be different, more like an adult party. And I was going to be in charge of everything, from making the food to deciding on the music. I wanted it to be perfect. I'd even started reading some of those slick home magazines — the ones I normally avoid like the plague — looking for tips on "holiday entertaining."

"Cool," said Stacey.

"That's great," murmured Mary Anne.

"Excellent." Claudia didn't look up from her beads.

Stacey was the only one of the three who really sounded psyched. I felt like smacking myself on the head. What a jerk! Of course the other two wouldn't be excited about a party. Mary Anne had just broken up with her boyfriend. And Claudia, well, for one thing, she and Stacey weren't exactly getting along. And Stacey would be sure to bring Jeremy to the party, which wouldn't help. I could see it all now. What was the point of a fabulous party if my friends weren't going to enjoy it?

I sighed.

Oh, well. I was going to go ahead with my plans anyway. My BSC friends weren't the only ones I was going to invite. And with luck, Claudia and Stacey would work out their issues before the party rolled around, and Mary Anne would be that much more used to not being a couple with Logan. The party could still be a success.

I checked Claudia's clock. Five fifty-three. Would the meeting ever end? This had to be one of the longest half hours of my life.

The phone rang two more times, once with a job request from Dr. Johanssen and once with a call from a girl in Claudia's math class who needed that day's homework assignment.

Finally, *finally*, the clock clicked to six. "Meeting adjourned!" I cried, jumping to my feet. I couldn't wait to leave.

Stacey seemed to feel the same way. " 'Bye!" she said, sprinting for the door.

Mary Anne and I said good-bye to Claudia. She seemed happy to be left with her beads. "Are you still coming over for dinner?" Mary Anne asked me as we left Claudia's house.

I'd almost forgotten that she'd invited me. "Sure," I said. "I'm looking forward to it." I was, too. It would be nice to spend some time hanging out with Mary Anne. At least there was no awkwardness between us.

But I can't say it was like old times either. It was strange to have dinner at Mary Anne's temporary house, which is next door to Claudia's. For one thing, it's weird to be back on Bradford Court with her, on the street where we both grew up. Also, this house just felt unfamiliar. It's oddly empty, since Mary Anne's family lost so much in the fire. And there are all these boxes around, things they salvaged from the fire but haven't unpacked. The boxes will probably sit there until Mary Anne's family moves into the new house they're creating out of their old barn. The smell of smoke still clings to the boxes. At dinner, Mary Anne's stepmother, Sharon, looked tired and sad, and her dad seemed preoccupied.

After we ate, Mary Anne and I hung out in her room for a little while. We talked about school and about the situation with Stacey and Claudia, but I had a feeling there was something else on her mind. Finally, it came out.

"So, who's Logan's partner for that biography project?" she asked, trying to sound casual.

"Rachel," I answered.

Mary Anne nodded.

"Does that bother you?"

"Why should it?" She raised her eyebrows. "He's a free agent now. He can hang out with anybody he chooses."

"He didn't choose," I reminded her. "Ted did."

"Oh, right. Anyway, I really don't mind. I know you probably think I'm having second thoughts about breaking up with Logan, but I'm not. It's just weird. Not to talk to him, I mean. We used to talk all the time. Now we probably wouldn't have anything to say to each other anyway. But it still feels weird. And it's strange knowing he'll be talking to somebody else."

She didn't have to add that the "somebody else" was a girl we never really liked. I knew it must be hard for her. We talked a little longer and then Watson came by to pick me up.

"You had a phone call," my mom said as soon as I walked into the kitchen. She handed me a slip of paper. "Cary wants you to call him back." A phone number was written underneath his name.

This was *not* my favorite day.

I really didn't feel like calling him back, but curiosity got the better of me. What did he want, anyway? I dialed the number on the paper. The phone rang twice and then somebody picked up. But he or she didn't say anything. "Hello?" I said tentatively.

"Who's this?"

I recognized Cary's voice. I should have known. Who else but Cary Retlin would answer the phone without answering it? "It's Kristy," I said.

"Yes?"

"You called *me*," I said.

"Not this time."

I wished I could reach through the phone line and smack him. "Come on, Cary, what do you want?"

"A truce."

"A what?"

"A truce," he repeated. "Look. We don't need a repeat of that gym-class thing. We got in a huge amount of trouble over that. I think we should work together this time. I mean, I know you annoy me to no end, and for some reason I seem to annoy you too. But I think we can reach an agreement, can't we? Just to make Ted happy."

I was still bristling from "you annoy me" — in what way could I possibly annoy *him*? — but I had to admit that Cary's idea was a pretty mature concept. What could I do but agree?

We made plans to interview each other and various family members. We even talked a little about other sources we could use. Our conversation was surprisingly . . . normal.

After we hung up, I pulled out the fiction list Ted had given us. I wanted to start thinking about which book I would read. The list looked interesting, and I marked several titles to check out further.

Little did I know how much trouble that list was about to cause.

❋ Chapter 4

Over the weekend, I spent some time at the library looking at books from Ted's list. By Monday morning, I'd narrowed my choices down to two. I was going to read either *The Outsiders*, by S. E. Hinton (everybody I know has already read it and loved it), or *The Red Pony*, by John Steinbeck, which I've heard is really good but sad. I was hoping to have a moment to talk to Ted before class, to see if he could help me choose which one to read.

I had also made up a list of questions for my first "interview" with Cary. We'd decided to meet after school that afternoon, and I wanted to be ready. Most of my questions were pretty basic. I had realized that I really didn't know much about Cary Retlin. And in a weird way, I was starting to feel interested in learning more.

I was still thinking over my questions as I headed for English class. As I walked through the hall, I noticed clumps of kids talking excitedly and looking upset. I wondered what was up. Had somebody been suspended? Or was it news from outside the school, for instance, something about the space shuttle launch? I didn't have time to stop and find out, not if I was going to talk to Ted before class.

I hurried along and arrived a few minutes before the bell rang. But Ted wasn't sitting alone at his desk as I'd hoped. Instead, he sat on the edge of it, surrounded by a group of students. The kids looked as upset as the ones out in the hall — and Ted looked even worse. What was happening? I approached the group, but I couldn't tell what they were talking about. I heard, "It's not fair" and "How can they do that?" but nothing that told me what was going on.

Finally, Ted stood up. He looked tired and sad, and I couldn't begin to imagine what was wrong. "You kids had better head to your next class," he said. "Go on, now. We'll talk some more another time."

The crowd broke up. One girl looked as if she were about to cry. "What is it?" I asked her. She just shook her head.

By then other kids from my class were drifting in. There was a buzz of conversation. Everybody knew something was wrong.

"Okay, folks," Ted's voice rose above the noise. "Let's all take a seat. I have a feeling there are lots of rumors floating around. Maybe I can clear things up a bit."

"So it's true?" Jeremy asked.

Ted held up his hands. "Hold on," he said. "Let's just wait until everybody's here and seated. Then I'll try to explain."

Just then, Cary came in the door and headed for Ted. He stuck out his hand for a shake. "I'm behind you, man," I heard him say.

Behind Ted? What did that mean?

"Thanks," Ted replied. Then, as Cary took his seat, Ted moved to the front of the room and asked for our attention.

Everybody fell silent instantly, and all eyes were on Ted.

"I don't know how to say this," said Ted, "but I may not be your teacher for much longer."

"What?" Logan sounded outraged. "Why not?"

The buzz of conversation started all over again. Ted held up his hands. "I think some of you may have already heard that there has been a call for me to be suspended or fired or punished in some other way."

"What are you talking about?" The words popped out of my mouth before I could stop them.

"I'm talking about the fact that some parents of kids in my classes do not like the book list I handed out on Friday. They object to some of the titles on it. In fact," Ted continued, "they're so angry about the books that they're making a point of asking the school administrators to make sure I can't hand out a list like that again."

This was unbelievable. I mean, we were talking about *books*.

"I want to say right away that I still stand behind these books." Ted held up the list he'd handed out. "If there are books on this list that you do not want to read, and that your parents do not want you to read, that's fine. That's your choice. All you have to do is find a book that you *do* want to read and that your parents consider appropriate. There is something for everyone on this list."

"My parents don't tell me what to read and what not to read," said a girl named Jessica.

Ted smiled at her. "That's great," he said. "Personally, I don't think parents should censor their kids' reading. But all I'm saying here is that you do have a choice. There are books on this list that nobody could possibly find objectionable." Ted sighed. "At least, I think there are."

I glanced around the room. Whose parents had complained? I couldn't imagine. Then my glance fell on a girl named Merrie. Merrie Dow. She has long blonde hair that she wears in two little-girl braids, and a very serious face. Suddenly, I remembered that her mom, Bertha Dow, was once involved in trying to ban some books from the Stoneybrook Public Library. She had picketed the library and written letters to the editor of the *Stoneybrook News*.

Merrie met my eyes. Then she lowered hers and blushed. Bingo! Bertha Dow must be behind this.

I felt sorry for Merrie. She looked miserable, and I couldn't blame her. If her mother became responsible for destroying the career of one of the best teachers we'd ever had . . . well, let's just say it wasn't going to do much for Merrie's popularity.

I glanced around and noticed a couple of other kids looking at Merrie. I guess I wasn't the only one who knew about her mom.

"What are you going to do?" somebody asked Ted.

He shrugged. "There's not much I can do. I've

contacted a lawyer, and I've made my position clear to the SMS administration. It's up to them to make the next move." He frowned. "What that will be, I can't guess." Ted put the list back on his desk. "For now," he said, forcing a smile, "I'm going to go on teaching. So, how are you coming with your biography projects? Any questions?"

We talked about interview techniques and other research methods for the rest of the class. But Ted's heart didn't seem to be in our discussion, and I couldn't blame him. I knew he must be feeling just terrible. I mean, he was facing the loss of his job. Over something ridiculous too. I told myself not to worry. They wouldn't really fire him — would they?

As we left class that day, I noticed that Cary looked almost as glum as Ted had.

"Come on," I said. "They can't really fire him for this."

"Sure they can. Teachers are fired all the time for the wrong reasons."

I realized then that Cary liked — and respected — Ted as much as I did. And I had to admit that made me respect Cary more.

For a few hours, anyway. Until our interview.

After school, Cary and I met in the library. We'd agreed to take turns interviewing each other that afternoon. He was waiting in one of the easy chairs near the window when I arrived. He watched, one eyebrow raised, as I sat down and pulled a reporter's notebook out of my backpack.

"What?" I asked.

"I didn't say anything," he replied, grinning.

Cary was Cary again. That eyebrow, that maddening way of making you feel like a fool.

"Don't you believe in taking notes?" I asked.

He shrugged. "I have a pretty good memory. So do you want to go first or should I?"

"Go ahead," I said. "Ask me anything." He didn't scare me.

Cary leaned back in his seat, put his fingertips together, and closed his eyes. "Who is the real Kristy Thomas," he mused. "And how do we plumb the depths of her being?"

" 'Plumb the depths'? Where did you come up with *that*?" I asked.

He just grinned. Then he started firing questions at me. "Who's your favorite Beatle? When you were six, what did you want to be when you grew up? What was the name of your first pet?"

"What?" I asked. "Favorite Beatle? What does that have to do with anything?"

"Just answer, please," he said. "I have my own methods."

"Um, Paul, I guess. He wrote a lot of good songs, according to my mom. And she says he was always the cutest."

Cary nodded, but he didn't write anything down. Then he asked me a whole bunch of other questions. I answered them as well as I could, even though some of them were pretty weird. Like the one about what I thought aliens looked like. I couldn't figure out how he was going to write my biography based on questions like that.

Things went from bad to worse when I started asking him questions. Let me just say right now, for the record, that Cary Retlin never gives anything close to a straight answer. Check out some of the responses he gave to questions I asked him:

Q: Where were you born?
A: In a hospital.
Q: In what state?
A: A state of innocence.
Q: What's your first memory?
A: I can't recall.

Ay-yi-yi. I'm sure you can imagine how I felt. Basically, I wanted to throw him out the window, even if we *were* only on the first floor.

How was I ever going to put together a biography of this incredibly irritating human being?

If I couldn't pry answers out of him, I was going to have to count on other sources. Starting with Cary's family.

❋ Chapter 5

The next day everybody at school was talking about what had happened to Ted. By then all the kids had heard about it. And man, were the rumors flying.

"Did you know that some of those books are totally X-rated?" I overheard that on the lunch line. As if it weren't enough to have to face a plate of beef stew that looked like something your dog threw up, I had to listen to nonsense like that.

"Mr. Morley's lawyer is going to pay off the school so they won't fire him," I heard in the hall near the gym.

"Merrie Dow's mom doesn't let her read anything except the Bible."

And, finally, "I heard Mr. Morley was in prison once."

Oh, please. I have never seen a place where rumors pass around more quickly than at SMS. I guess some kids are just so bored that they have to make up stuff like that. I wish they'd get a life.

I tried not to listen to or participate in too many discussions about Ted. At this point, we just had to wait and see what the school was going to do. There was nothing to be gained by talking it over endlessly.

Cary seemed to agree with me. Neither of us brought up the subject as we walked to his house after school. It was the day we'd chosen for me to go home with him and interview his family. I had tried to prepare a list of good questions. Whether or not I'd have any good answers by the end of the day was still up in the air. Way up.

Instead of talking about Ted, we talked about basketball (he thought the Knicks were looking great so far this season), current events (a flood in Arkansas, the latest news from Washington), and dogs (his family is looking for a new one). It was the most normal conversation I've ever had with Cary Retlin. Which felt very strange. It was hard to relax into it. I kept expecting him to lift that eyebrow and come out with some sarcastic remark.

When we arrived at his house, nobody else was home. Great. I'd come to interview his family, but there wasn't another Retlin in sight.

"My brothers will be home any minute," Cary said. "Ben usually stops by the elementary school to walk Stieg home." He opened a cupboard. "Are you hungry?"

I was, but I said I wasn't. I'd thought about it and decided I probably wouldn't be able to trust any snack Cary whipped up.

He made himself a peanut butter and jelly sandwich and ate it while I watched (feeling hungrier than ever). Just as he was putting his plate in the sink, his brothers burst through the door.

"Hey, Ben. Hey, Stieg. You guys have met Kristy before, right?"

Cary's brothers are cute. Ben (short for Benson) is eleven. Stieg is eight. Both of them seem smart and well adjusted. Neither of them seems to take after Cary in the sarcasm department.

"Kristy would like to interview you," Cary told them. "Remember? For that project I told you about?"

The boys nodded. "I'll go first," Stieg volunteered.

"Great," I said.

"You can talk in the den," said Cary, leading the way to a small room filled with shelves of books. I took a seat in a comfortable leather easy chair, and

Stieg sat opposite me on a cushy-looking red couch. "Have fun," said Cary as he closed the door behind him. And I could have sworn I saw that eyebrow do its thing in the last glimpse I caught of his face. Uh-oh.

Stieg looked at me expectantly.

I cleared my throat. "Okay, let's see," I said, glancing down at the list of questions I'd prepared.

"Do you want to hear about the time Cary stole something?" Stieg asked, a mischievous look in his eyes.

"Uh, sure." I picked up my pencil. This sounded interesting. I hadn't known Cary had a criminal past.

"It was back in Illinois," Stieg said. "We were at the supermarket with my mom. I was watching Cary, but he didn't know it. So I saw when he put a pack of gum into his pocket."

A pack of gum! I'd been expecting something a little more unusual. Lots of kids have stolen packs of gum. "Did you tell on him?" I asked.

"I didn't have to," Stieg replied. "My mom saw him too. She made him give the gum back and apologize. She was pretty embarrassed, I think. You know, because my dad used to be a policeman."

I'd forgotten about that. Once, when we thought Cary might be a suspect in a local burglary, the BSC members had tried to learn a little bit about his background. We hadn't found out much, but we did discover that his father had been a police officer until Cary was about eight. Now Mr. Retlin is a locksmith. I scribbled a couple of notes. "Anything else?" I asked.

"He always hogs the remote when we're watching TV," Stieg said. "And once, when we were little, he pinched me so hard I cried." Now that he'd started, Stieg couldn't seem to stop reporting Cary's misdeeds. "He cut all the hair off this girl's doll one time. And he broke my mom's favorite vase."

I nodded. "Go on." I had actually stopped taking notes, but I was tickled by Stieg's recitation. I had the feeling he was trying to get back at his big brother for something. For what? Oh, probably just for being a big brother. I know how that is. You envy your older brothers for all the privileges they seem to have. And you store up grievances. It's only natural to try to even the score when you have a chance.

Finally, when Stieg started to wind down, I tried to ask him some of the questions on my list. But he wasn't interested in answering. He'd had his own agenda for our interview, and he was satisfied now that he had revealed all of Cary's "crimes." Eventually I realized that I'd learned all I was going to learn from Stieg. I thanked him and asked him to find Ben for me.

A few minutes later, Ben was sitting on the red couch. He wasn't nearly as open as Stieg had been, but he wasn't as evasive as Cary had been the day before either. He answered my questions straightforwardly without adding any extra comments.

When I asked about the town they'd lived in back in Illinois (it was called Oak Hill), he told me its population and principal industries. He explained why his dad had left the police force (the work was too dangerous) and said that Cary had been a star on his Little League team when he was younger.

His answers were complete but not very interesting. Except for one. When I asked why his family had moved away from Illinois, Ben clammed up. "Ben," I asked again. "Why did you leave Oak Hill?"

"I can't tell you that," he answered, folding his arms across his chest.

It was clear that there was no changing his mind, so I moved on to another subject. But that answer — or nonanswer — nagged at me. I wondered if there were some big family secret about the move.

When I'd finished with Ben, I asked him where the bathroom was. He sent me upstairs. When I was done there, I walked down the hall, peeking into the Retlins' bedrooms.

I know, I know. It's not nice to snoop. But hey, I was on a mission. Some biographers go through the trash their subjects throw out! Talk about snooping. Compared to that, glancing into a bedroom or two was nothing.

One room had bunk beds. That must be Ben and Stieg's. The room across from it had one big bed and two closets. That must belong to Cary's parents.

The room at the end of the hall had to be Cary's. I walked quietly toward it. I thought I'd stand at the open door and peek in, just to get a sense of what Cary's room would be like. But then something came over me — a terrible urge. I went back down the hall and glanced out a window. Cary was outside, filling a birdfeeder in the backyard. Yes! He was busy. I hurried into his room and eased the door shut behind me. I think you can tell a lot about a person from his room, and I wasn't about to pass up the chance to check out Cary's. In the back of my mind I knew it was wrong. But I couldn't resist.

Oh, yeah. This was Cary's room all right. Who else would have a poster of the universe with a little

YOU ARE HERE arrow pointing to Earth? Who else would have a weird painting of clocks melting all over the place? (Claudia told me later that it was probably by a guy named Salvador Dalí, who was famous for "surreal" paintings.) Or one of a man with a big green apple for a head? (That was by Magritte, according to Claudia. Also a surrealist.)

A bulletin board over his desk was covered with funny postcards, bizarre newspaper headlines ("Goat Responsible for Power Outage," said one), and cutout pictures of movie monsters. It was quite a display.

I turned around slowly, taking in the room. His green plaid bedspread and curtains looked relatively normal, but the lamp on his bedside table was pure Cary. It was a miniature skeleton with a lightbulb held high in one hand.

I looked back at the bulletin board. I had to admit that it was pretty cool. Then my glanced dropped to his desk. On top was an open notebook. I figured Cary must have started his homework while I interviewed his brothers. I bent over to look at it, wondering if he'd figured out how to do the math problems we'd been assigned that day.

It wasn't his homework.

It was more like a journal.

And once I started reading, I couldn't stop.

> I admit it: Sometimes
> I still regret the things
> I did that got me kicked
> out of school. I mean, I
> liked my town. I just
> didn't like the people.
> What a bunch of phonies!
> So I loaded up my computer
> and... now I'm exiled. I'm
> a thousand miles away
> from my old life. But
> I still think about it
> every day.

I felt a chill run through my body.

Okay, spare me the lecture. I know it was wrong to read Cary's private thoughts. And I knew it then. Still, all I wanted to do at that moment was to read more. But I was scared to turn the page. Would Cary know I'd been snooping?

Just then, I heard footsteps in the hall. They were coming toward the room I was in. I froze.

The footsteps came closer.

And I couldn't make myself move.

Chapter 6

"Kristy?"

I was speechless. I couldn't answer. It had taken all my presence of mind to jump away from the desk just before Cary walked into the room. When he appeared, I was staring at a poster that showed two hands, each in the act of drawing the other. If that sounds strange, it was. But it was actually kind of neat. According to the caption on it, the artist's name was M. C. Escher.

Cary looked puzzled. "What are you doing in here?" he asked.

I stared back at him blankly. What could I say? I didn't really have any good reason for being in his room.

"What?" I asked, stalling for time.

Cary glared at me. "Kristy, why are you in my room?"

"This is your room?"

He rolled his eyes. "No, it's Spider-Man's. Of course it's my room."

"Oh."

"I know I may be in danger of repeating myself." Cary took a step closer to me. "But why are you in my room?"

"This is a really cool poster," I said desperately, gesturing toward the picture of the hands.

"M. C. Escher." Cary spoke as if he knew the artist. "He was Dutch, born in eighteen ninety-eight. He had some wild ideas."

"I noticed," I said.

"I have a book of his drawings," said Cary. "Want to see?"

"Sure." Somehow, my diversionary tactic had worked. Cary seemed to have forgotten that he'd caught me snooping in his room.

I glanced at the desk and the open notebook. I shuddered, thinking of the words I'd read.

I'd always known Cary was *different*. He was too smart for his own good, he was arrogant, he was sly, and he was tricky. But I'd never imagined him to be a dangerous hacker. A criminal. (Well, once I did imagine that he might have stolen those jewels. But only briefly.)

My head was spinning. Had Cary really been kicked out of his last school?

"Yo, Thomas!"

I blinked. Cary was staring at me, that eyebrow lifted in a quizzical way. He was holding an oversized book in one hand and waving the other in front of my face.

"Are you in there?" he asked. "Or have aliens sucked out your brain again?"

"Aliens," I answered with a weak smile.

"Do you want to see the book?"

"Sure." We sat down on the floor and Cary opened the book.

"This is one of my favorites," he said, turning pages until he found a picture that showed, at first glance, a bunch of white birds. "See, when you look closer, you see that the birds' shadows — the dark spaces between the birds — are actually *other* birds, black ones," Cary said. He was gazing at the picture, running his finger over some of the details.

I stared at his profile. He didn't *look* like a criminal. Other than the eyebrow and the smirk, he looked like your ordinary, everyday eighth-grade boy. And, more than anything, I wished I could still think of him that way. I glanced at his desk again and felt my stomach turn over. How could I have read his personal journal?

I hadn't meant to. I really hadn't. But it had been lying open, right under my nose. Who *wouldn't* have taken a peek? I wouldn't have started reading if I'd known it was his journal. I swear. But I didn't know what it was until it was too late.

"This one is really cool," Cary continued, flipping pages. "See how the stairs go all around the building? You think you're looking at a 'down' staircase, and then suddenly it turns into an 'up' staircase." He shook his head. "This guy amazes me," he said. "Can you imagine what kind of mind he must have had to think of these things?"

What about Cary's mind? What kind of warped, twisted mind was lurking underneath that dirty-blond hair? Sure, lots of kids joke about causing chaos with their computers. But how many of them actually *do* it?

I gasped.

Suddenly I realized something.

My biography project had just become a *lot* more interesting.

I was probably the only student in any of Ted's

classes who was going to turn in a biography like this. The story of someone kicked out of school because of a secret past!

"Don't you think?" Cary was staring at me again.

"Um?" I said alertly.

"I said, don't you think this is cool?" Cary asked, showing me a picture of a bunch of weird little lizards that moved by curling themselves up and rolling along.

"Way cool," I agreed. "Coolest thing I ever saw."

Cary looked satisfied. "Not everybody appreciates Escher," he told me. "Maybe I've underestimated you."

I managed to smile. "Maybe you have," I said. Maybe everybody had. But when they saw the biography I was going to turn in —

Screeech! Put on the brakes, Kristy.

Turn in? Biography? It hit me like a ton of bricks. There was no way I could write about what I'd just discovered. How could I? I wasn't supposed to *know* the things I knew. They were private. Confidential. Cary wouldn't tell me about them, not in a million years. And — I remembered the way Ben had clammed up — nobody else in his family was going to either. Which meant I had to act as if I'd never read those words. *Sometimes I still regret the things I did that got me kicked out of school. . . .*

Aaughh!

Here I was, sitting on the biggest secret in SMS history, and I had to keep it to myself.

"Something wrong, Kristy?" Cary was giving me a strange look.

I glanced down and noticed that my fists were clenched tight. Had I groaned out loud?

I shook out my hands. "Not a thing," I said. "Not a thing."

"You're acting kind of weird," Cary remarked. "But maybe that's normal for you. I guess I'll find out more when I interview *your* family." He raised the eyebrow.

"Could be," I said. Suddenly I didn't have the energy for any more banter.

Cary gave me a closer look. "No, you really are acting weird. What's up?"

"Nothing." I shook my head, resisting a powerful urge to look at his desk. I had to get out of that room before I gave myself away. "Um, I'm just a little distracted by all the other homework I have to do. I think I should head home."

"If you say so." Cary shrugged. He closed the

Escher book and stood up to replace it on his shelf.

"Sorry," I said. I didn't know exactly what I was apologizing for. Maybe it was for reading his private journal and learning his innermost secrets. Or maybe it was just for leaving early.

"No problem," said Cary. He looked a little bewildered. "So, then, we'll go to your house next time?"

"Oh, right," I said. "Sure. How's Thursday?"

"Works for me, I think." Cary walked to his desk as if he was going to check his schedule. I held my breath. Would he notice that his journal was lying out in plain sight? Would he guess that I had seen it, *read* those incredible few sentences?

If he did, he didn't show it. He just made a little note on his calendar and turned away from his desk.

I let out my breath. "Okay, then," I said.

"Okay," he echoed.

"So, I'll see you."

"Not if I see you first," Cary replied, sounding more like himself.

"Right," I said, inching my way out the door. " 'Bye!" I ran down the stairs. Suddenly I couldn't wait to leave that house. I blasted past Ben and Stieg, who were coming out of the kitchen, grabbed my backpack, and fled out the front door.

I walked home quickly, thinking hard. What a ridiculous situation! How had this happened? I didn't even want to know the things I knew. On the other hand, as long as I knew them, I sure would like to be able to write about them. But I couldn't write about them, because I wasn't supposed to know about them. Cary didn't know I knew, and if he found out, he might go berserk. Maybe he'd try to hack into my own computer. He might be capable of anything.

It wasn't easy to act casual at dinner that evening, but I did my best. I think Watson noticed something was up when I passed him the ketchup. "I asked for the salt," he commented, giving me a puzzled look. "But thanks anyway."

I don't know what we talked about over our hamburgers and salad, but I'm pretty sure I didn't contribute anything too meaningful. Afterward, I helped clear the table, then left Sam and Charlie to the dishes, since it was their turn. I took the portable phone into my room and dialed Mary Anne's number.

"Hello?"

"It's me," I said. "I, um, had some ideas about my Christmas party. Do you think it would be too much to decorate the punch bowl with lights?"

I didn't really have any interest in talking about my party — not at the moment, anyway. I had other things on my mind. But how could I bring up the real issue?

Finally, I presented it as a hypothetical case. "Mary Anne," I blurted out, interrupting her, "what if you accidentally found out something private about someone? Something that person didn't want you to know? Do you tell him you know?"

Good old Mary Anne didn't seem fazed by my sudden switch in subjects. "Depends," she said. "Do you have a reason for saying something? Or could you maybe forget the thing you found out?"

"Forget it?" I asked slowly. "I don't think so."

"In that case, honesty is probably the best policy."

Mary Anne is usually right about these things. But I wasn't convinced. Honesty may be the best policy where most people are concerned, but I was dealing with Cary Retlin. And Cary Retlin is definitely not like "most people."

❀ Chapter 7

The next day I spent the morning avoiding Cary. I had the feeling seeing him at school was going to be awkward after what I'd read in his journal. How could I face him?

For everybody else, it was an ordinary Wednesday. For me, it was something else. I was the only person at SMS who knew that we had a criminal in our midst. As I walked around the halls, I reflected on how I would feel if I were booted from *our* school. I mean, it's not my favorite place in the universe. Maybe I'd want to celebrate if I were told to go somewhere else.

But I didn't think so.

I'd miss it. I would miss the front hall, with its display cases full of trophies. I would miss the main bulletin board, all covered in notices and posters. I'd miss the auditorium, my locker, and yes, even the cafeteria.

After all, I'd spent an awful lot of time in that building over the last few years. In a way, it was like another home to me.

Yikes. If any of my friends had known what I was thinking, they'd have thought I had gone nuts. And maybe I had. I felt tense and stressed out, like a cat on its way to the vet.

Mary Anne noticed. (Mary Anne always notices things like that.) "Are you okay?" she asked when we were at our lockers between classes.

"Sure." I gave her a false smile just as the bell rang.

"We'll talk later," she said. I hadn't fooled her for a minute.

My next class was English. It was time to face Cary. I ran into him around the corner from my locker. "H-hi!" I said brightly.

"Hello to you," he said in an amused tone. "Feeling all right?"

"Feeling excellent. And you?"

"Fine, thanks." I think he noticed that I was a little nervous around him. Especially when I almost walked into the door of our classroom.

"It's customary to *open* the door," Cary said, grinning at me as he reached for the doorknob.

He lost his grin as soon as he looked inside. I followed his glance.

Mr. Taylor, our principal, was standing at Ted's desk.

And Ted was nowhere to be seen.

Immediately I forgot about my problems with Cary.

"This isn't good," Cary muttered. "It's not good at all."

We took our seats.

The second bell rang, and the last kids trickled in and sat down. Then Mr. Taylor began to speak.

"Good morning," he said. He was twisting his hands together and sort of squinting.

"Good morning," we chorused.

He took a breath. "You may notice that your regular teacher, Mr. Morley, is not here today," he said.

"Oh, really?" said Alan Gray.

Mr. Taylor gave him a Look and continued. "Mr. Morley is going to be taking some time off while the administration of this school investigates the charges being leveled against him."

Now Mr. Taylor sounded as if he were reciting a speech he'd memorized. I wondered if he'd said the same thing to all of Ted's classes. And I wondered if the kids in every class had stared at him in shock the way the ones in my class had.

Mr. Taylor was looking toward a back corner of the room. Merrie Dow was in the front. I could tell he was trying hard not to look at her while he talked. But every kid in the class was looking at her.

"This is most likely a temporary measure," Mr. Taylor added hurriedly. "We hope to avoid too much disruption to your learning cycle here in English class." He stopped twisting his hands and shoved them into his pockets. Then he cleared his throat. "Any questions?" he asked.

My hand shot up. He gave me a slight nod. "Are you telling us that Ted was suspended just for handing out a list of books?" I asked.

Mr. Taylor looked taken aback. "Well, yes," he admitted. "I suppose you could put it that way. Mr. Morley has indeed been suspended, pending investigation. And the book list he gave you is part of the reason."

"Part?" asked Cary. He hadn't bothered to raise his hand. "What do you mean, 'part'?"

Mr. Taylor sighed. "Let me explain," he said. "The *content* of the list — the books that are on it — is only part of the problem. The other part is that Mr. Morley apparently neglected to have his list approved by the head of the English department. That's standard procedure in this school."

Alan Gray was waving his hand. "But that's not fair," he cried. "Ted came here all of a sudden, to fill in for Mrs. Simon. He might not have known about that rule."

"Be that as it may," said Mr. Taylor, "the rule does exist."

Cary's hand shot up. Mr. Taylor glanced at him. I could tell he would rather not call on Cary, but he didn't have much choice. He'd asked for questions, after all. He nodded at Cary.

"What do *you* think about the situation?" Cary asked.

Mr. Taylor took a step backward. "What I think is only part of the picture," he declared after a pause. He frowned and looked into the back corner of the classroom again. "I will say that I believe Mr. Morley meant no harm. He is a respected teacher, and this matter will receive a fair hearing. I fully intend to make sure of that."

Cary turned around in his seat and glanced at me. I could tell by his look that he was thinking the same thing I was: Mr. Taylor was not very happy about what had happened. There must have been tremendous pressure to suspend Ted.

Mr. Taylor wasn't the only adult at SMS who was unhappy about Ted's suspension. After class, as I walked to my locker, I could see little groups of teachers in the halls. They were talking quietly among themselves, but not quietly enough. I heard whispers of "ridiculous," "scary — it could be me next," and "what about the First Amendment?"

That last remark caught my interest. I'd learned about the Constitution in seventh grade, but I couldn't remember exactly what the First Amendment said. During study hall, I went to the library to check it out.

Mr. Counts, the librarian, was only too happy to help me. First he showed me where to find a copy of the Constitution so I could read the First Amendment. "Congress shall make no law," it says, "respecting an establishment of religion, or prohibiting the free exercise thereof; or abridging the freedom of speech, or of the press; or the right of the people peaceably to assemble, and to petition the Government for a redress of grievances."

"It's the part about freedom of speech and of the press you'll find most interesting," Mr. Counts said. "That is, if you're wondering about Mr. Morley's rights."

"I am," I told him.

"You may find this interesting too." Mr. Counts pulled a book out of a stack on his desk. "This is the most recent *Resource Guide* for banned books. It's put out every year by the American Library Association."

He handed me the oversized book, and I flipped through it. There was a list of every book banned or challenged in the past year, as well as a long list of books titled "Some People Consider These Books Dangerous." That list included all the books that have been banned or challenged over the years, from 387 B.C. to the present!

"Some of those books have been burned," Mr. Counts said. "Others have been taken off library shelves or attacked publicly by people who wanted to keep them from going on the shelves in the first place."

"Wow," was all I could say. "There are a lot of familiar titles on this list." Some of them were on the list Ted had given us, including both books I was thinking about reading. And I remembered some of them from the last time I was exposed to bookbanners: *To Kill a Mockingbird, A Light in the Attic, The Adventures of Huckleberry Finn*. But the list went on and on, naming books I never would have thought of as "dangerous" in any way. "*In the Night*

Kitchen?" I cried. "How could anybody have a problem with that?" It's a great picture book, right up there with *Goodnight Moon*.

"You probably don't even remember," Mr. Counts told me, smiling a little. "But in some of the pictures, the little boy is naked."

"Oh, please," I said. I continued to leaf through the book.

"I can't lend you this copy," said Mr. Counts. "But if you'd like to borrow last year's edition I'd be glad to check it out for you."

I didn't have to ask where Mr. Counts stood on the Ted Morley question. It was clear that he thought the suspension was wrong.

I didn't know anybody who thought it was *right*. When we talked about it at the BSC meeting that afternoon we all agreed (even Stacey and Claudia agreed, for once) that the suspension was way out of line. And at dinner that night my mom and Watson made it clear that they supported Mr. Morley all the way.

"I'm going to write a letter to the newspaper," my mom declared. "Somebody has to take a stand against this garbage." She showed me a letter in that day's paper — a letter from Bertha Dow. In it, Mrs. Dow claimed that Mr. Morley was a "corrupting influence on the youth of Stoneybrook," and that the "trash" he was promoting as appropriate reading was going to drive us to "immorality."

Watson was angry too. "I'm going to call the school tomorrow," he said.

Ordinarily, I might have been embarrassed if my parents had made a public fuss. But in this case, I was all for it. As my mom said, "Sometimes you have to be loud to defend what you believe in."

I only hoped I could do something to help.

❀ Chapter 8

"What a day!" Cary leaned back in his seat and closed his eyes.

We were on our way to my house after school on Thursday. Cary was sitting next to me on the school bus, in the spot usually taken by my friend Abby. She calls our bus the Wheeze Wagon, because it sounds as if it's taking its last breath. I was waiting for Cary to make some snide remark about that, but he didn't.

Maybe he was just too tired to be clever or sarcastic. I couldn't blame him. I felt wrung out myself. It had been a long, long day at school. The news about Ted's suspension was all anyone could talk about, and the rumor mill was working overtime.

"Did you hear about that group of parents who went to see Mr. Taylor?" I asked. Apparently Mrs.

Dow and a few other "concerned parents" had paid Mr. Taylor a visit.

"Hear about them?" Cary raised an eyebrow. "I *heard* them. It was hard not to. They were yelling at the tops of their lungs when I walked by the office."

I wondered if Watson had called the school yet. I made a mental note to ask him to inform Mr. Taylor that Mrs. Dow did not represent the majority of SMS parents.

I shook my head. "I wonder how this is all going to end," I said. "What a mess."

Cary agreed. "It's a big waste of time. And it could foul up Ted's record forever. It might even cost him a job sometime."

I glanced at Cary. I wondered if he related to Ted somehow. For example, did Cary have a "fouled-up" record because of what happened at his old school? Had it followed him here to SMS? That seemed doubtful. I'd never seen the teachers or Mr. Taylor treating him differently than they did any other kid. Maybe Cary's parents — or possibly a lawyer? — had been able to keep it off his permanent record.

It was on *my* Cary Retlin record, though. I couldn't forget about it. I'd blocked my computer with a stack of books that morning, knowing he'd be coming to my house after school.

I was also a little nervous about Cary's interviews with my family. Not that I had anything to hide. I was just hoping against hope that nobody he talked to would volunteer any especially embarrassing stories about me. I didn't need Cary — let alone everyone in school — knowing about some dumb thing I'd done when I was seven.

I had mentioned the interviews to Watson and my siblings, who would be home that afternoon. (Watson works at home a lot.) In the spirit of fairness, I had tried not to coach them too much. But I had made sure to remind them about some of my better moments, in hopes they'd mention those events to Cary.

I'd spent some time reminiscing with David Michael about all the great times we'd had together while I was coaching him in softball.

I'd reminded Watson about some of my community-building projects, like the BSC's work with the residents at Stoneybrook Manor, the local retirement home.

Sam and Charlie would talk (I hoped) about my accomplishments as BSC president, including some of my best fund-raising ideas.

And I was just trusting that Karen and Andrew would be their usual talkative selves, and that they'd want to boast about me generally, since they're proud of their older stepsister.

I had done what I could do. The rest was up to my family. When Cary wrote my biography, would I come out looking like a champ — or a chump? I'd have to wait and see.

This was the first time Cary had visited my house, and as we walked to the front door I could see that he was impressed. "Nice place, Your Highness," he said. "Are the palace guards on a break?"

I rolled my eyes. "It's not *that* big," I said.

"No, it's just a little hut. I can see you live the simple life."

I ignored him. "Come on in," I said, opening the door. "But don't expect much. I've given the servants the day off."

Cary grinned at me. "In honor of my visit? You shouldn't have."

I brought Cary into the kitchen and offered him a snack. As we were eating our nuked burritos, various members of my family began wandering into the room. First was Sam. Then Karen showed up. Charlie popped his head in, and soon after that Watson stopped by, along with David Michael.

I introduced Cary to everyone and told them — in front of him — to answer any questions he asked.

"Even if they're about your disgusting personal habits?" asked Sam.

"*Especially* if they're about my disgusting personal habits," I said.

"This sounds interesting," Cary remarked. "Maybe I'll start with you, Sam."

"Excellent," Sam answered. "What can I tell you about my beloved little sister?"

"Let's see," said Cary, pulling a notebook out of his backpack. "I have a few questions about her early life." He turned to me. "Would you excuse us?" he asked.

"I haven't finished my snack yet," I pointed out. "I'll just sit here quietly, okay? Not a word. Pretend I'm not here."

Cary shrugged. "Whatever." He turned to Sam. "Now, tell me a little about Kristy as a baby. Was she cute? Did she have any hair when she was born? How much did she drool?"

"Hey!" I said. "What does drool have to do with anything?"

Cary glared at me. "I thought you were going to sit quietly."

"Oh, right," I said. I pretended to zip my lip. "Go on."

Cary looked back at Sam.

"Well," said Sam, "as I remember, she was a little bruiser. She'd grab my finger and hold on so tight I could have swung her around. But the other thing about her was that she was constantly — and I mean *constantly* — wetting herself."

"I was a *baby*!" I cried. "That's what babies do!"

Cary swung around. "That's it," he said. "I don't care if you've finished your burrito or not. You're out of here. This is supposed to be a biography, not an *auto*biography."

What could I say? Cary'd left me alone when I'd interviewed his brothers. I had no choice but to return the favor. As I left, I shot Sam a Look that was supposed to mean, "If you say one more embarrassing thing I'll kill you."

Sam just grinned back at me. I had the feeling he knew exactly what I meant, and that he planned to ignore me completely.

Oh, well. It was out of my hands. I headed upstairs to my room, figuring I might as well start on my homework.

An hour or so later, just as I was making headway on a paper for social studies class, there was a knock on my door. "Anybody home?"

It was Cary's voice. Did I want to let him into my room? I glanced around. Fair was fair. I'd seen *his* room. More of it than he knew. "Come in," I called, after checking to make sure nothing embarrassing was in sight.

"Well, well, well," said Cary, glancing around as he entered my room. "I guess I now know just about all there is to know about the real Kristy Thomas."

"You wish," I said.

"I know all the good stuff." He raised that eyebrow and added the smirk. "Like how you used to call your baby dolls Eenie and Beenie."

"Big deal," I shot back.

"And how you once cried because you thought the moon was going to crash into your backyard."

I shrugged. If that was the worst he'd heard, I wasn't worried.

The smirk was still there. "Then there's the time you had an 'accident' on Santa's lap," he continued. His eyes were sparkling.

I drew in a breath. Did I want my classmates to know I'd peed on Santa? I shook myself. I could handle it. After all, they were kids once too. I made my face blank to show Cary I didn't care.

"And, of course, there's the Spaghetti Episode," Cary said. I noticed that he was watching my face carefully. He was hoping for a reaction.

I tried to hold myself back, but I couldn't. "You're not going to write about *that*!" I cried.

"Are you kidding? Of course I am. It's the most hilarious thing I've ever heard."

"Cary Retlin," I said, "you better not — "

He held up his hands. "You said you had nothing to hide, didn't you?"

I might have said it, but I guess I didn't mean it. The Spaghetti Episode is my secret. I'm not even going to reveal it here. "Cary," I said warningly.

"I think I'll lead off with it." He stroked his chin.

That was too much. "Look," I said desperately. "That was a long time ago. It's ancient history."

"I think it explains a lot," said Cary. "About your personality, I mean." He was being playful, but suddenly I couldn't take it anymore.

"Well, at least I didn't get kicked out of school!" I blurted out.

"What?" Cary was staring at me. "What are you talking about?"

"I know why you had to move to Stoneybrook," I said. Suddenly the whole mood had changed. The joking was over.

"Why I had to — " Cary looked puzzled. He paused, and I could practically *see* him figuring it out. Then a shadow passed over his face. "You read my notebook?" he asked.

He looked hurt. That surprised me. I would have expected him to look angry, and he was starting to. But the pained look was unexpected. I felt a knot form in my stomach. What I had done was wrong, so wrong.

"I — I didn't mean to," I started to explain. "It was on your desk — "

"Don't bother," he said coldly. "I can't believe you did that, Kristy. How could you?"

"I'm sorry — " I began.

He made a motion with his hand, cutting me off. "You know what? Now I know the real Kristy Thomas. And she's a total jerk."

He walked out of my room, slamming the door behind him.

❋ Chapter 9

I didn't sleep much that night. I tossed and turned, brooding about the situation with Cary. I would spend half an hour convincing myself that what I'd done wasn't so bad. After all, the notebook had been lying in plain sight. And I would never have started reading if I'd known it was a journal. And . . . well, you can imagine the rest. I had plenty of excuses. But they didn't hold up well. For the next half hour, I would berate myself for being such a snoop, for betraying Cary's trust, for throwing his past in his face during a stupid argument. I could see both sides of the situation. And I knew that from Cary's side, what I had done was unforgivable.

For awhile, at least.

I was hoping that Cary would come around eventually. I mean, don't get me wrong. He'll always be my archenemy. But it wasn't any fun when he was so mad at me. The truth was that I'd come to see that Cary wasn't such a bad guy.

As long as you kept him away from the computer.

Really, other than the criminal thing, Cary was an okay guy. Sure, he liked to antagonize my friends and me, and he was always acting superior and smug. But underneath it all, he was, well, an interesting guy.

Other than the criminal thing . . .

That was pretty hard to forget.

But what I'd done to him was even harder.

Before homeroom on Friday morning, I looked for Cary in the halls. I guess I wanted to try to apologize again. But I didn't have the chance, because Cary was nowhere in sight. Was he avoiding me? Probably. I didn't see him after homeroom either. Or between first and second periods, or second and third. Normally our paths cross at least a few times during the morning, so I knew he must be making an effort to keep his distance.

I hadn't talked to any of my friends about what had happened. How could I? If I did, I'd spread Cary's secret even further. Mary Anne could sense that something was wrong, but after she'd asked twice and I hadn't answered, she knew better than to push me to talk.

Finally it was time for English class. Cary couldn't avoid me any longer. When I walked into our classroom, I noticed that he was sitting in a new seat, across the room from the row we usually sit in. He didn't look up when I entered.

Okay, I thought. *Be that way.* I took my usual seat.

"Hello, class," said the woman who was sitting at the teacher's desk. I'd barely noticed her when I'd arrived, partly because she was a completely unnoticeable person. She was medium height with medium-brown hair. She wasn't fat and she wasn't thin. She was wearing a beige skirt, a lighter-beige blouse, a darker-beige jacket, and brown shoes. "I'm Ms. Dewey, your substitute," she said in a thin, colorless voice. She smiled uncertainly. "I'll be teaching this class until — until . . ." she broke off. "Well, for awhile, anyway."

We all just sat there and looked at her. She seemed so absolutely boring that not even Alan Gray could think of anything funny to say.

This is who they gave us in exchange for Ted Morley? I thought.

I felt like crying.

"So!" Ms. Dewey smiled brightly. "Let's all take out a piece of paper, shall we?"

"What for?" called a voice from the back.

Ms. Dewey adjusted her beige glasses. "Well, for an assignment. I thought we would spend our class time working on a short essay today."

"We?" That was Cary. "Are you going to write one too?"

"What's it supposed to be about?" asked Cokie in a tired tone. "What we did over Thanksgiving vacation or something?"

We're used to substitutes who give meaningless assignments. And normally it doesn't bother me much. But for this woman to come along after I'd become used to Ted . . . well, let's just say it was disappointing.

"Oh, no," said Ms. Dewey in answer to Cokie's question. "That would be silly. I thought we would do something more in line with the biography unit you're working on. For example, I thought we might write about 'My Favorite Historical Figure.' Her fingers made little quotation marks in the air as she announced the title. Then she smiled hopefully at us.

Everybody groaned.

Her smiled disappeared. Her hands fluttered as she tried to figure out what to do next. "I think if you just try, you might find it interesting," she began.

"Not!" called out Alan.

"I second that," yelled another boy.

"Oh," Ms. Dewey said, almost to herself. Now she was twisting her hands. I felt sorry for her. After all, it wasn't her fault that Ted had been suspended. And it wasn't her fault that she was the beige-est, most boring person in the universe.

I felt sorry for her — but I felt sorrier for myself and for the rest of the class. It wasn't fair! What had we done to deserve this? No Ted. A boring substitute. A beyond-boring assignment.

Wait a minute.

Was that true? Was there really nothing we could do? Were we going to let people like Mrs. Dow decide what our English class would be about?

I sat straight up in my seat. And without even raising my hand, I started to talk. "You know," I said, "this just doesn't seem fair. I mean, where's Ted? Why isn't our teacher here?"

Ms. Dewey looked shocked. "Why, he — he — "

I waved my hand. "No, I know *where* he is," I said. "What I mean is, why are we letting it happen?"

Kids were looking at me. They either thought I was crazy — or right. "Look," I continued, turning around to meet as many eyes as I could. "We should *do* something about this. We shouldn't just sit here and take it."

Kids were still looking at me. I had their attention, all right. But did I have their support?

"We can't let a few people tell our school what to do. If we disagree with their ideas, we need to say so. We need to let our voices be heard!" I paused and looked around.

There were a few seconds of silence in the room. Then Claudia spoke up. "Kristy's right," she said. "If we let them punish Ted for this, what could happen next? What if an art teacher is fired for showing us pictures of naked statues or something?" A few kids giggled, but Claudia ignored them. "I'm serious. This issue isn't going to go away. We need to stand up for freedom of speech."

That's right," a voice said from the other side of the room. "This is about freedom. We can't just sit here and let our rights — and Ted's rights — be taken away." It was Cary!

I felt so much better knowing I had the support of two classmates. I glanced at Ms. Dewey and realized something interesting. I had her support too. She was still standing in front of the class, but she'd folded her arms and she wore a slight smile. The fact that she had let me and the others speak must mean that she agreed with me.

I met her eyes and smiled at her. Maybe she wasn't completely beige after all.

Two rows over, Merrie Dow cleared her throat. Then she tossed her braids back and started to speak. "I think," she began in a tiny voice.

I braced myself. Were we about to hear from the opposition?

Merrie cleared her throat again and spoke a little louder. "I think Kristy's right. If we don't speak up, nobody will know we even care. And we do. Or at least I do."

I stared at her. Merrie wasn't known for being a rebel. As far as I knew, she usually went along with whatever her mother thought.

She continued, her voice growing louder with every sentence. "Mr. Morley was — *is* — one of the best teachers I've ever had. He makes learning exciting and fun. And I don't think there's a thing wrong with that reading list. If there are books on there that you don't want to read, don't read them! It's your choice."

I realized my mouth was hanging open as I stared at Merrie. The rest of the class looked stunned too.

Merrie stopped speaking and looked down at her desk. A blush reddened her cheeks.

"You go, Merrie!" yelled Alan, breaking the silence.

The rest of the class broke into an excited buzz.

"I don't know," Cokie said above the din. "I mean, what if my parents don't want me to read some of those books?" She looked worried.

"Then you don't have to read them," chorused three or four kids together.

Cokie nodded. "I guess that's true," she admitted. Then she grinned. "But I might anyway."

Ms. Dewey had taken a seat at her desk by then. Now she stood up again. "All right," she said, holding up her hands for quiet. It took awhile, but finally everybody stopped yelling. "It sounds as if you have a new project on your hands. I hear a lot of energy and a lot of good intentions. But what are you going to do next? Exactly how are you going to make your voices heard?" I gaped at her. Ms. Dewey was *definitely* not all beige. "From what I understand, there will be an open administrative hearing next Monday to discuss Mr. Morley's case — "

Cary didn't let her finish. "Then we need to be there," he said. "And we need to round up as many other kids and as many parents as we can. There's strength in numbers."

We spent the last ten minutes of class planning our strategy. Ms. Dewey took notes on the board. "I suppose I could be suspended for this," she said with a little laugh at one point. "But I'm only a substitute. Let's consider this a lesson in, let's see, organization!"

By the time the bell rang, we had a plan. And I had been elected our class representative to state our case at the meeting. I walked out of the classroom feeling terrific. I caught Cary's eye and smiled at him — but he didn't smile back. He might have supported me in the classroom, but that didn't mean he had forgiven me.

Chapter 10

As I walked out of school toward my bus later that afternoon, Cary fell into step beside me. *All right,* I thought. *Maybe he's coming around after all.*

"That was pretty great, what happened in English class today," I said tentatively. "I mean, that everybody was so psyched about helping Ted." I added that last part hastily, since I didn't want him to think I was complimenting myself for having started the ball rolling. He nodded. "I just hope we can round up enough people for that meeting," I went on, filling the silence he'd left. "It would be awesome if we could fill the room with Ted's supporters." I glanced at Cary. He didn't seem to be listening anymore. "Don't you think?" I added desperately.

"Look, Kristy," Cary said, a little too loudly. He pressed his lips together and frowned. "It's like this.

What you did was absolutely despicable. Invading someone's privacy like that is just about the lowest thing you could do."

"But — "

He held up a hand. "This isn't an argument, Kristy. I'm telling you how I feel. And how I feel is that I have no desire at all to talk to you. None."

"Oh." I took a step backward.

Cary sighed. "But I can't afford to fail this English assignment. So I've drawn up a list of questions I need you to answer for my biography." He stopped and bent to rummage around in his backpack. Then he pulled out a sheet of paper and handed it to me without meeting my eyes. "This is all I need to finish things up," he said. "You may have some final questions for me too."

"I — I . . ." I was so shocked I couldn't speak.

"If you do, you can just write up a list for me. I'll fill in the blanks and pass it back." He shouldered his backpack. "See you," he said. Then he walked off, disappearing into the crowd of kids waiting for their buses.

I stared after him. Yikes. I'd learned something. Playing archenemies had been annoying. But being real enemies was horrible. I felt sick.

I glanced at the list in my hand. He'd probably

thrown in a bunch of gag questions, just to be a smart aleck. But no. Every single question — I scanned the list quickly — was serious, straightforward, and, to tell the truth, kind of boring. Not at all like the Cary I knew.

I let my hand drop to my side and stood staring off in the direction Cary had gone. For a second, I had a wild hope that he would reappear around the corner of the building, grin at me, and say, "Gotcha!"

But that wasn't going to happen.

That afternoon I once again looked over the questions Cary had given me, but I didn't have the heart to work on answering them. Instead, I lay on my bed for awhile, staring into space and trying to work out some way to make things right.

I hadn't figured anything out by the time our BSC meeting rolled around, but I was still trying. Charlie teased me about my silence during our drive to Claudia's house. "I can practically hear the gears moving inside that head of yours," he said to me. "Careful, you don't want to wear out your brain!"

I ignored him. I wasn't desperate enough to ask his advice.

Yet.

In Claudia's room, I tried to forget my troubles

and concentrate on running the meeting. But it wasn't one of the club's best days. After I'd called the meeting to order Mary Anne asked an innocent question.

"How's the biography project going?" She reached into the box of Mallomars Claudia was passing around and pulled one out.

Now, what was I supposed to say to *that*? "Well," I said slowly, "it's kind of . . . actually, Cary and I have hit a little snag." Obviously, I couldn't go into any of the details. I didn't know what I'd say if she asked any more questions.

Fortunately, Claudia jumped in.

Unfortunately, what she said made Stacey feel rotten.

"It's going great for me," said Claudia. "Jeremy is so interesting!" She reached out for a Mallomar. "I mean, today I found out that he once swam with dolphins down in Florida or somewhere. He said it was one of the most meaningful experiences of his life. It was as if he was communicating with the dolphins. Isn't that awesome?"

Stacey did not look happy. "He never told me that," she said.

"I'm sure he would have," Mary Anne put in. "Eventually, I mean."

Stacey just glared at her. "The most meaningful experience of his life, and he tells somebody else before he tells me?" She was holding a big pretzel Claudia had passed her, and she broke it in half without seeming to notice.

"*One* of the most meaningful," I pointed out. "Not *the* most meaningful."

"Oh, big difference," said Stacey. "Right. So all I have to do is ask him what was the *most* meaningful experience, and then I'll know more than her."

Claudia blushed. "Actually," she said, "he kind of told me that already."

Stacey looked as if she wanted to stomp out of the room. But she kept her cool. "Oh?" she said, raising her eyebrows. "And what was it?"

Claudia's blush grew deeper, but she was smiling. "Um, I'm not really supposed to tell."

"Oh, that's just terrific." Stacey threw up her hands.

I decided the time had come to change the subject. "So, about my Christmas party," I began, trying to sound cheerful. "The invitations are in the mail!"

Stacey, who had still been glaring at Claudia's profile (Claudia refused to look at her), glanced at me. "You invited Jeremy, right?" she asked.

"Right," I said with a sinking feeling. Oh, man.

If Claudia and Stacey couldn't deal with the Jeremy issue when he wasn't even in the room, what was it going to be like when the three of them were at a party together?

"I just hope he doesn't spend the whole evening whispering secrets into his *friend's* ear," she said frostily, avoiding Claudia's eyes.

"I won't go near him, if that's what you want." Claudia looked angry now. "If you're so insecure about your relationship, I'll just stay away."

"Insecure? I'm not insecure. I just don't like it when — "

Luckily the phone rang just then. For a few minutes we were forced to act professional. By the time I'd set up a sitting job with the Pikes, Stacey and Claudia had simmered down.

"So, Kristy," Mary Anne asked with a falsely casual note in her voice, "did you invite Logan?" She bit into her second Mallomar.

"Not yet," I replied. "I was waiting to talk to you about that. Do you think it would be okay? Or would it be awkward?"

"You mean you might not invite Logan?" Claudia interrupted. "That would be weird, since a lot of his other friends will be there."

"I know. But it has to be okay with Mary Anne." I looked at her. "Is it? Okay, I mean?"

Mary Anne glanced down at the Mallomar she was holding. She looked as if she'd just lost her appetite. "Do you think he'll come with a date?" she asked.

I shook my head. "It's not that kind of party. At least I don't want it to be. I think people will just come on their own."

"Not that he couldn't date if he wanted to," Mary Anne added, with a shaky smile. She was still holding the Mallomar. She reached for a tissue from the box on Claudia's night table, wrapped the cookie in it, and threw it away. "Sorry to waste that. I just wasn't hungry anymore." She took a deep breath and turned to me. "It's okay if you invite him," she said. "I'm a big girl. I can handle it."

I nodded. "All right, then," I said.

As I looked around the room at my friends, I realized that I wasn't the only one with problems. It wasn't an easy time for any of us.

❄ Chapter 11

1. Who was your third grade teacher?
2. How old were you when you learned to walk?
3. How many cousins do you have, and what are their names and ages?
4. What is your favorite color?

Eeesh. I looked down at Cary's list of questions. Could they be any more boring? *Oh, well*, I thought. *At least it won't take me long to answer them.* It didn't either. I whipped through the whole page in under an hour. Then I wrote up a similar list for Cary. It was just as boring as his, because I couldn't ask the one question that mattered most: What did you do to be kicked out of school? When the list was done, I rode my bike over to his house to drop it off.

I was hoping he might be home so I'd have another chance to talk to him, but the house was deserted. I left the list in his family's mailbox and headed back home.

Sunday evening seemed to stretch on forever. All I could think about was the meeting about Ted, now less than twenty-four hours away. I'd told Watson and my mom about it, and they'd promised to come. I tried to make some notes about things to say at the meeting, but I couldn't concentrate. I was too mad.

All day Monday I felt as if I were marking time. Every hour was just part of the countdown to the big meeting.

Finally, the moment arrived. My English class had agreed to gather in the hall and walk into the meeting together, so I looked around the crowded entrance until I spotted Jeremy and Alan. As I headed for them, I saw Watson and my mom arrive and join some of their friends. Jeremy looked tense.

"What's up?" I asked.

He glanced to his right, and I followed his eyes. There was Merrie — and Mrs. Dow. They were arguing in hushed tones.

"But I promised I'd sit with my friends," Merrie was saying in a strained voice.

"Friends? Those are not the kind of friends you

should have, young lady," said Mrs. Dow. "You're sitting with me."

Merrie looked pale. Slowly, she shook her head. "No, I'm not," she said. "I'm sorry," she added in a whisper. Then she turned and joined the boys and me. Mrs. Dow gaped after her.

I reached out to touch Merrie's shoulder. "Good for you," I said quietly. "You really stood up for yourself."

She tried to smile. "Thanks."

Jeremy nodded to her. "That couldn't have been easy," he said sympathetically.

Alan just smiled and kept quiet, which was probably a good thing. It wasn't the time for one of his wisecracks, and for once he had the sense to see that.

I glanced at my mom, who was standing near the door with Watson and another couple. I spotted the SAY NO TO CENSORSHIP button on my mom's lapel and smiled to myself. I was proud of her, and I knew I was lucky to have a mom who felt the way I did about issues like this one.

Soon the rest of our class arrived. The crowd around the entrance had grown, and I tried to guess how many of them were on Ted's side and how many were not. It was impossible to tell by looking at people, except for the small knot of men and women standing with Mrs. Dow. They were all talking angrily, and several of them were carrying briefcases bulging with, I assumed, materials to support their case.

"We'd better go in," Jeremy said, "if we want to find seats together. Looks like it's going to be crowded in there."

He was right. We were able to grab a row in the auditorium (I saved seats for Mary Anne and Stacey, who had promised to come), but by the time everyone had filed in, the room was packed and most seats were taken.

I sat between Jeremy and Claudia. Cary took a seat at the other end of the row, but I tried not to let it bug me. I was here to concentrate on helping Ted.

The noise level in the auditorium was incredible. If you think a cafeteria full of middle-school students is loud, you should try an auditorium full of angry community members. Everybody was talking at once while they waited for the meeting to begin.

". . . no right to subject our children to filth . . ." I heard on one side.

". . . a decent man, and he doesn't deserve to lose his job over . . ." I heard on the other.

The buzz in the room became even louder when Ted walked onto the stage, accompanied by a man and a woman in business suits. "They're lawyers from the teachers' union," Jeremy said. "I heard they'd be with him."

Now Mr. Taylor was walking onto the stage, along with our assistant principal, Mr. Kingbridge, and several teachers, including most of the English department. They filed in, looking very serious, and took seats on the other side of the stage from Ted. A large podium stood between Ted and everyone else from SMS.

"This looks more like a trial than a meeting," I whispered to Claudia. She nodded with a little shiver.

Mary Anne and Stacey arrived just before Mr. Taylor stood up at the podium. They slid into their seats as he called the meeting to order. "I'd like to welcome you all to this meeting," he said. "The administration of SMS is pledged to consider the needs and concerns of the Stoneybrook community. An issue has been raised concerning the conduct of Mr. Ted Morley, and we are here to discuss the case and hear from those involved: that is, Mr. Morley himself, the head of the English department, the parents of this community, and any students who wish to speak."

I felt my heart race when I heard that. I did "wish to speak," but the size of the crowd in the auditorium was intimidating. Would I really be able to stand up for what I believed in, in front of all those people?

Fortunately, I didn't have to do it right away. Mr. Taylor invited Ted to speak first. "I believe that Mr. Morley has a right to explain and defend his actions," he said, waving Ted up to the podium.

Ted stood for a moment, looking out at the crowd. Then he took a deep breath. "Thank you all for coming," he said. "It's good to see so many people in this community taking an active role in the education of their children."

The crowd murmured. I had a feeling the protesters hadn't expected Ted to be so diplomatic.

"I'd like to apologize, first of all," said Ted, "for not submitting my reading list for the approval of the English department. I honestly did not know this was required. At my last teaching post, which was at a private school, teachers made assignments at their own discretion. My introduction to SMS was rushed, and if I was told of this requirement I forgot about it. I do apologize for this." He paused, cleared his throat, closed his eyes for a second, and began to speak again. "I do not, however, apologize for the content of that list."

There was a stirring in the auditorium, and several people began to speak at once. "Save our children!" called out one woman.

Mr. Taylor stood up and joined Ted at the podium. "Everyone will have a chance to speak," he said, leaning closer to the microphone. "I must ask that you hold your comments until you are called on." He waited for a moment until the buzz had died down. Then he nodded to Ted and took his seat again.

"I don't have a lot more to say," Ted continued. "Just that I stand behind every book on the list I handed out. I would also like to remind everyone that not one of the books on that list was mandatory reading. Students had complete freedom of choice in terms of what they decided to read, including choosing a book *not* on the list."

"It's still a choice between smut and filth!" yelled out a man in the third row.

"It's time to let us speak!" shouted the woman sitting next to him.

Mr. Taylor stood up again as Ted took his seat. "As I said before, everyone will have a chance to speak. But the next person we'll hear from is Ms. Breer, head of the English department. Please give her your attention and respect."

Ms. Breer stood up, looking a little nervous. "I

just want to go on record as saying that the department values Mr. Morley's classroom expertise," she began.

A loud hiss came from somewhere near the back of the auditorium. Mr. Taylor rose halfway to his feet and glared out from the stage, and the noise stopped.

Ms. Breer gave him a grateful glance and continued. "It's true that Mr. Morley may not have understood the protocol we follow regarding reading lists. Mrs. Simon's early departure was a surprise to all of us, and we may not have been able to brief Mr. Morley as thoroughly as usual." She looked down at the notes she was holding, bit her lip, and went on. "I would also add that if Mr. Morley *had* presented his list to me, I would have approved it."

Some of the protesters jumped to their feet and started yelling. Other people, Ted's supporters, began to applaud.

Ms. Breer stepped back from the podium. Then she walked quickly to her seat. Mr. Taylor stood again and held up his hands. "Please, please," he said. "Can everyone please quiet down? Let's continue in a civilized manner." He peered out into the auditorium. "I call now on Mrs. Bertha Dow, who will represent her group, Parents for Decency."

Merrie was sitting two seats away from me, on

the other side of Jeremy. I could almost feel her cringing, and I shot her a sympathetic look. Jeremy gave her a little shoulder hug.

Mrs. Dow climbed the steps to the stage and took her place behind the podium. "I want to say, first of all," she began, "that we are not here to destroy anyone's name or create any sort of community rift. We simply care about our children's moral education. It is up to us, their parents and teachers, to bring them up to be decent, respectful adults. Children are not born with values; they learn them. And some of the books on this list," she waved a piece of paper in the air, "do nothing but subvert the values we hold most dear."

A cheer rose from one section of the auditorium.

Mrs. Dow went on to point out page numbers that, she said, contained instances of "excessive violence, obscenity, negative role models, and immorality" in some of the books on Ted's list. Books like *The Catcher in the Rye* and *Homecoming*.

I could hardly believe my ears. I watched Ted closely as Mrs. Dow was speaking and saw him wince as she tore into the books on his list.

When she finished, there was a huge burst of applause — and a scattering of boos. I glanced at my mom. I knew she wouldn't boo, because she would consider that rude. But I couldn't help agreeing with the people who were letting Mrs. Dow know how they felt. How could anyone sit still and let her talk that way about great books?

"I'll now call on those who have come to support Mr. Morley," said Mr. Taylor after the noise had died down. He glanced at a paper in his hand. "Mrs. Rioko Kishi?"

I saw Claudia's mom rise and walk toward the stage, and I reached over to squeeze Claud's hand. "I bet she'll be great," I whispered.

She was.

Mrs. Kishi is the head librarian at the Stoneybrook Public Library. She must have had a lot of experience with this issue, because she came prepared. She spoke simply but powerfully about the First Amendment and what it means. She mentioned court cases that have supported the right of the American people to free choice. And she read several quotes that made my spine tingle. I asked her about them later and wrote some of them down. "Freedom of thought and freedom of speech in our great institutions of learning are absolutely necessary . . . the moment that either is restricted, liberty begins to wither and die. . . ." That one was by someone named John Peter Altged. Another one, from Supreme Court Justice William O. Douglas, was, "Restriction of free thought and free speech is the most dangerous of all subversions. It is the one un-American act that could most easily defeat us." (Right on, William O.!)

The issue was bigger than I had ever imagined. I felt exhilarated to be part of the debate.

Mrs. Kishi left the stage and took her seat amid more buzzing and shouting. Then Mr. Taylor was standing behind the podium again. "I understand that Mr. Morley's students would like to speak," he said.

Gulp. My exhilaration vanished, to be replaced by panic. It was my turn to talk.

❀ Chapter 12

I knew I should stand up, but I couldn't make my legs work. I felt incredibly hot. The sweater I was wearing was making my neck itchy. And I couldn't seem to breathe easily.

Jeremy nudged me. "Go ahead, Kristy," he whispered. "You can do it!"

I met his eyes, and he smiled and nodded. *No wonder Claudia and Stacey like him so much*, I thought. Jeremy is a genuinely nice guy.

Claudia patted my shoulder. "Just tell them what we think," she reminded me. "Nothing to it."

I looked at her with raised eyebrows. "Nothing to it?" I asked. "Do you want to do it?"

She shook her head vehemently. I had to laugh. That relaxed me enough to unparalyze my muscles, and I stood up. I began the long walk to the stage.

I saw heads turn to look at me as I went by. My mom gave me a big thumbs-up, and Watson smiled and nodded encouragingly. I saw Stacey's mom sitting a few rows down, and Mary Anne's dad and stepmother. Most of my teachers were there, and lots of kids I knew from other classes.

As I passed the rows where the protesters were sitting, I shivered a little. Their glances were cool, and some of them even looked angry. I had a feeling they thought kids shouldn't have any say in matters like these.

I met Mrs. Dow's eyes just briefly, but then she turned away to whisper something to the woman sitting next to her. Probably something about me, about the way my classmates and I were corrupting her little girl.

That walk down the aisle seemed to take forever. Finally, though, I reached the steps to the stage. I climbed them carefully, since I didn't especially want to trip and fall on my face in front of all those people. As I stepped onto the stage, I found myself in front of Ted. He met my eyes and gave me the tiniest smile. It was almost as if he were saying, "Don't sweat it, Kristy."

Seeing Ted up close seemed to blast energy into

my body. I felt ready to take on that whole auditorium of people. Shoot, I could have spoken in front of the U.S. Congress at that moment.

I strode to the podium and thanked Mr. Taylor. I pulled a folded piece of paper out of my back pocket and flattened it out on the podium. I'd finally written up a few notes for myself in study hall that afternoon. But when I glanced at them, I realized I didn't need them. It would be easier just to speak from the heart.

Breathe, I reminded myself. I looked out at the sea of faces staring at me and took a long, deep breath. Then I glanced at Ted again, smiled at him, and began to speak. "Did any of you ever have a really good teacher?" I asked the audience. "The kind who inspires you to do your best? The kind who helps you learn to think in new ways and helps you enjoy learning?" I paused. "Ted Morley is that kind of teacher. He is one of the best teachers I've ever had, and I know that many of my classmates feel the same way. He respects his students as people, and he makes us excited about using our minds."

I stopped to take a breath. The auditorium was very quiet. People were listening to me.

"All I want to say is that I — and my class-mates — think it would be a real shame to lose a teacher like Mr. Morley. And in our opinion, he hasn't done anything wrong. None of us felt pressured in any way to read a particular book on that list. He made it very clear that we had a choice. Personally, I don't think there's anything wrong with any of those books, but if I did, or if my parents did, I could have chosen not to read them."

Suddenly, a voice rang out from the audience. "This girl does not speak for all the children in Mr. Morley's classes!" a woman shouted.

It was Bertha Dow.

I swallowed hard. I glanced at Mr. Taylor, but before he could do anything, somebody else spoke up.

"Yes, she does."

It was Merrie. She was standing, and she spoke clearly and firmly. She faced the stage, not her mother.

Awesome. Merrie was full of surprises.

Next to her, Jeremy began to clap. Then Claudia joined him, then Alan. Soon everybody in our row was applauding, and then the applause spread throughout the auditorium. I heard a few whistles and cheers as well.

Mrs. Dow sat in her seat, facing forward. She did not glance back at Merrie or even show that she had heard her daughter's statement. Stony-faced, she ignored the applause.

Out of the corner of my eye, I saw Mr. Taylor begin to stand up. I nodded to him. It was time to wrap things up.

"I just want to say one more thing," I went on. "I would like to ask the administration to consider the feelings of Mr. Morley's students. We don't want to lose him as our teacher!"

I stepped back from the podium. After a second, I heard Claudia shout, "Go, Kristy!" And someone began to clap. Soon the auditorium was again filled with cheers and applause. I heard a few boos in the mix, but what could I expect? It wasn't as if I were going to change the protesters' minds. (Not that I wouldn't have liked to.)

I walked off the stage, smiling at Ted as I passed him. He grinned at me. "Thanks," he mouthed.

I was back in my seat in a flash. The walk that had seemed so long in one direction took just moments going back. The faces I passed — mostly smil-

ing, a few frowning — were a blur. The applause ta-
pered off as I worked my way down our row. Mary
Anne stood up to give me a hug as I passed, and
Claudia held up her hand for a high five. "Nice
work!" whispered Jeremy.

I felt so relieved — and incredibly proud of
Merrie. I leaned past Jeremy to smile at her. "You
were great," I whispered.

She smiled. "Thanks," she murmured, shrugging.
"I just said what I felt."

"Me too," I answered.

Next I glanced down the row, hoping to catch
Cary's eye. It would be nice to know he approved of
what I'd said. But he was staring straight ahead, listening to the next speaker, a student from one of
Ted's other classes. Every other kid in our row
looked back at me and grinned or gave me the
thumbs-up, but Cary ignored me completely.

I stopped listening to the kid at the podium. I
wanted to patch things up with Cary, but how?
Should I let him read *my* journal?

No way.

I don't write in my journal often, and when I do
I'm usually really upset about something. So it's
pretty personal.

What if I let Cary ask me anything — *anything* — and promised to answer him honestly? That might work. I'd have to think about that one.

The meeting went on. One person after another spoke, saying the same things over and over again. First one of the protesters would speak, then one of Ted's supporters. Finally, Mr. Taylor looked at his watch and announced that it was time to end the meeting. "Let's take a ten-minute break," he suggested. "The administration will need to consult about what our next step will be."

Most people stayed in their seats during the break, and the auditorium hummed with conversation. Mr. Taylor, Mr. Kingbridge, and the teachers who were sitting with them pulled their chairs into a tight circle and talked in low voices. A couple of teachers from the audience joined Ted and his lawyers on their side of the stage.

I talked with Jeremy, Merrie, and Claudia until Mr. Taylor stood up and walked toward the podium again. He motioned for quiet, and the audience fell silent.

"We feel that we need more time to make a final determination in this case. It is not a matter we want to take lightly. A decision will be announced within a few days. Meanwhile, Mr. Morley will be reinstated to his position, pending final evaluation of his case."

For a second, I didn't understand what he meant. Then, a huge cheer went up, and I realized that Ted would be back in the classroom with us, at least temporarily.

Our side had won — for now.

❋ Chapter 13

"Okay, okay, that's enough!" Ted was blushing. "I mean it!" He held up his hands. "Thank you, really."

All of us — the entire class — were on our feet, applauding. It was Tuesday, the day after the meeting. And we were giving Ted a standing ovation. It wasn't planned. It happened spontaneously, because we were so happy to see him back in our classroom. I looked around at all the smiling faces in the room: Alan, Jeremy, Claudia, Merrie — and Cary. I hadn't seen Cary smiling in quite a few days, ever since that awful moment when he figured out that I'd read his journal.

My stomach turned over again at the thought of it. More than anything, I wished I'd never read those words. I hated knowing Cary's terrible secret. I hated that Cary was mad at me. And I hated the fact that the biography project had turned into such a mess.

Ted finally convinced us to stop applauding and take our seats. "Thank you," he said again. "I mean it. You can't begin to imagine how much I appreciate your support." He stuck his hands in his pockets. "I guess this situation is providing my classes with a lesson I didn't plan, about personal freedom and about the First Amendment."

Somebody in the back row gave a long whistle.

Ted grinned. "That's right," he said. "The First Amendment *rules*!" Then he grew serious again. "And I'm glad you're learning about it. But we have other things to learn, the things I was actually hired to teach. So I'd like to try to get back on track as quickly as possible. We have two big projects to work on — "

"Awww," called out Alan. "I was hoping you'd forgotten about those assignments."

"No such luck." Ted smiled and shook his head. "I fully expect to see both projects completed on time by every student in this class. I hope that you're making good progress. In fact, I'd like to meet with each biography pair sometime after school today." He held up a piece of paper. "Here's a schedule, with ten-minute time slots. Please consult with your partner and sign up as you leave class."

I glanced at Cary, but he didn't return my look. Oh, well. He couldn't ignore me forever. We were going to have to cooperate, if only for those ten minutes with Ted.

The rest of English class flew by. Ted went over the format for our biographies, reviewing basic concepts such as paragraphs, theme sentences, and conclusions. There wasn't any more talk about his suspension.

When the bell rang, I looked at Cary again. This time, he met my eyes. Reluctantly, he worked his way over to my side of the room. "What time is good for you?" he asked brusquely.

"Anytime," I said. "As long as I can catch the late bus home."

We walked to Ted's desk and waited for a chance to look at the schedule. "How's this?" he asked, pointing to a slot between Claudia and Jeremy and Logan and Rachel.

"Fine," I answered with a shrug.

He wrote in our names. "Catch you later, then," he said over his shoulder as he took off.

"Later," I echoed.

For the rest of the day, I tried not to think about Cary. Did that mean I paid attention in my classes? Well, not exactly. Instead, I daydreamed about my Christmas party. During math, I wrote down the names of every CD owned by my siblings and me. Then I narrowed down my choices, trying to pick music that everybody would like. That's not always easy, since my friends have pretty wide-ranging tastes.

During social studies, I pondered the important question of whether nachos or pizza would be better. Either way, I was also planning on serving chips and dip, plus brownies and these outrageous pecan cookies Nannie makes.

And, while I went through the motions of playing basketball in gym class, I thought of all the games I knew, from Scattergories to charades, trying to decide which ones would work to liven things up. I didn't want this to be one of those parties where everyone just sits around making awkward conversation.

The distraction worked. I was able to put Cary aside until the last bell rang. Once school ended, our meeting with Ted was only half an hour away. I decided to spend that time looking over my notes so I'd be able to report on my progress when we sat down for our meeting.

I found a seat in the library and pulled out the notebook where I was keeping the material I'd gathered about Cary. He'd given me the answers to my list of questions the day before, shoving the paper into my hands as we passed in the hall. I'd looked them over enough to know that he hadn't offered any surprising or interesting answers to my boring inquiries. Oh, well. I had the basic facts to work with, and that would have to be enough. But as I stared at the papers in front of me, I couldn't help thinking about the most important fact of all: Cary had been kicked out of his last school. And there was no way anybody but me would ever know.

"Hey."

I jumped a little in my seat. Cary was standing in front of me, holding his notebook loosely in one hand. "Ready?" he asked.

I checked my watch. It was almost time for our meeting. "I guess," I answered. He stood there silently as I gathered my papers together. So silently, in fact, that it made me nervous. I kept dropping things, first my pen, then my calculator, then a sheaf of papers. I picked them all up and shoved them into my backpack. When I finally stood up I couldn't take it anymore. "Cary, I'm sorry!" I blurted out. "How many times do I have to say it? I'm sorry, I'm sorry, I'm sorry. You can't believe how sorry I am!"

He just nodded.

I gave a huge sigh (I felt like screaming, but we were in the library, after all). "Well, thanks for writing out the answers to my questions," I said. "And maybe one of these days, if I'm patient, you'll start speaking to me again."

He raised an eyebrow. "Ah, but *which* one of these days?"

Yes! A weird answer. And the eyebrow. He was starting to sound like himself again. Maybe there was hope.

Claudia and Jeremy were just leaving as we arrived at Ted's room. They were talking happily, and I'm not even sure Claudia saw me as she passed by. I knocked lightly on the door.

"Come on in," said Ted. He smiled broadly as we entered. "Kristy, I want to thank you again for that marvelous speech you made. I was very moved by the things you said about me."

I felt myself blushing. "Well, they're true," I murmured.

"It wasn't easy to speak in front of that huge

crowd," he said. "My knees felt like Jell-O when I was talking."

"Kristy did a good job," Cary announced, taking me by surprise. "She said what all of us feel." He wasn't looking at me while he spoke.

"Thanks!" I couldn't believe he'd said that. But the way he was avoiding my eyes sent a clear message: He might give credit where credit was due, but he still hadn't forgiven me.

"So," said Ted. "Why don't you take a seat and tell me how your projects are going."

We each sat down in one of the chairs near his desk. Cary cleared his throat. "Things are going well," he said.

"Great." Ted smiled at me. "You agree with that?"

"Sure." I shrugged. "I have most of the information I need. Now I just have to put it together in an entertaining way."

"That's the trick," Ted said. "The facts are the easy part. The hard part is making them interesting."

Well, yes and no. One of the facts I knew was pretty interesting all by itself. But it was the one that was never going to appear in my finished paper.

"Have you been able to find many secondary sources?" Ted asked.

"I have," said Cary. "Kristy's pretty famous around these parts. I've found articles mentioning her, not only in the school paper but even in the *Stoneybrook News.*"

"Excellent." Ted nodded. "How about you, Kristy?"

"Well, Cary hasn't lived here very long," I said vaguely, looking down at my notebook. I was thinking that there was probably plenty about him in his hometown newspaper. But I wasn't about to mention that to Ted. "The interviews with his brothers were helpful, though."

"Good, good." Ted seemed satisfied, and I felt a little guilty. After all, Cary and I weren't being completely honest with him. "And the fiction part of the project? How's that going? Have you both chosen the books you want to read?"

I nodded. "I'm going to read *Homecoming,*" I said. "I hear it's really good." I'd ended up changing my mind about what to read at the last minute.

"I think you'll like it," said Ted. "How about you, Cary?"

"I'm reading *The Catcher in the Rye.* I've already started it. I think Salinger is an awesome writer."

"And a controversial one," Ted added with a little grin. *The Catcher in the Rye* was one of the books that seemed to make people like Mrs. Dow angriest. "Good fiction — and nonfiction — is hard to write, and sometimes even harder to accept."

Cary and I both nodded wisely.

"That's it, then," said Ted. "I think our time's just about up. I'm glad to know you're both on target with your projects."

He stood up and stretched as we gathered our things. "Speaking of Salinger," he said to Cary, "how's your novel coming? I think I saw his influence in the section you showed me."

"It's going okay," Cary muttered.

"I think it's terrific that you can write in notebooks," Ted went on. "I'm addicted to working on my computer myself."

Cary just kept stuffing things into his backpack. But I stared at Ted.

Novel?

Notebooks?

❋ Chapter 14

"*Novel?*"

I whirled around to face Cary as soon as the door to Ted's classroom had closed behind us.

He just looked at me.

"Cary Retlin, you answer me. Was that a novel I read?"

He shrugged. "Maybe it will be someday," he said. "Right now it's just a bunch of notes and stuff."

He was trying to act as if nothing unusual were going on. I could have wrung his neck. "I thought that was your diary!"

He shrugged again. "I never said it was." I saw a tiny half smile beginning to form on his lips.

That did it.

I narrowed my eyes at him. "You are a creep," I began. "You made me think — I can't believe — " I couldn't even spit the words out. "You know what?" I finally managed to say. "You're a jerk."

I turned and walked away as quickly as I could. I heard him call my name once, but I ignored him. At that moment, I had to put some distance between Cary Retlin and me.

I was steaming.

How could he have let me believe that he had been kicked out of his school? He must have thought it was unbelievably funny to watch me twist in the wind the past few days. This wasn't the first time that Cary had pulled a dirty trick on me, but it was by far the worst. This one wasn't funny.

I motored through the halls, not even noticing where I was going. Eventually I found myself out in the parking lot, where the late buses line up. I stood waiting in the cold, barely noticing that my hands were freezing and my ears were tingling. I thought again about that tiny half smile and stomped my foot.

You know what one of the worst things was?

He was right.

He had never said that what I'd read was a diary. And reading it in the first place was (as I'd already admitted a gazillion times) wrong on my part.

So he was right.

But I didn't care. I was too mad to care. And I knew that, right or not, he'd done it on purpose. He'd let me go around thinking horrible, terrible things about him, just for a laugh.

Well, ha-ha-ha. Very funny. Now he'd had his stupid, dumb joke. I looked like a fool, so he was probably satisfied.

Creep.

Jerk.

Booger-head.

(I know, I know. That's incredibly first-grade of me. But it's how I felt.)

I thought all these things as I rode the bus home, let myself into the house, made a snack, and ate it. I could not get over the fact that Cary had duped me.

When I'd finished my peanut butter and jelly sandwich, I headed upstairs to my room, still fuming about Cary. As I closed my door, I heard Sam and Charlie arrive home. I didn't go downstairs to see them. I needed to cool off before I could deal with anyone.

I threw my backpack on the bed and began to pull stuff out of it. My gaze fell on the notes for my biography. Ha! I grinned to myself. Biographies weren't always flattering to their subjects. What if I wrote the truth about Cary? Maybe it would help me work out some of my anger.

I sat down at my desk and turned on the light. Then I spread my notes in front of me, read through them one more time, and began.

CARY RETLIN: PORTRAIT OF A PSYCHOPATH
From a very young age, Cary Retlin was a rotten person. His first crime, the theft of a package of gum, may have seemed harmless. But it was only the beginning of a lifelong pattern....

I giggled as I wrote. I was starting to feel better already.

Cary's siblings are only too happy to testify to his selfish nature (see notes on hogging of remote control) and his endless cruelty (see notes on pinching, doll-hair cutting, etc.)...

Now I was on a roll. The world was about to meet the real Cary Retlin.

Cary may have been known as a baseball star back in his hometown of Oak Hill, Illinois...

I heard the doorbell ring downstairs, but I ignored it.

The truth, while shocking to some, must be told. Cary Retlin, the boy who makes a joke out of everything, is ...

There was a knock at my door. "Come in," I said.
"Hey."
It was Cary.
He was standing in my doorway, carrying a notebook and wearing a determined look.
I started to say something (something like, "Get *out* of my room!"), but he cut me off.

"Listen," he said. "I have something to say. The thing is, I understand why you're mad."

He did? I found that hard to believe. But I didn't bother to say anything.

Cary was pacing around my room, up and down along the windows opposite my bed.

"But you know what?" he went on. "It doesn't matter that the stuff you read was more fiction than fact. See, I write stories *instead* of writing a diary." He held up the notebook, a notebook that looked just like the one I'd read in his room. "And the plotlines of the stories aren't exactly the same as what happens in my life, but there are similarities." He saw my mouth open and put up a hand. "No, I did not get kicked out of school, or even suspended. But there is a lot of my life in these notebooks. And they aren't meant for people to read. Especially you."

"But — "

"No 'buts,' Kristy Thomas. Fact or fiction, you shouldn't have read it in the first place. And you know I'm right about that."

Of course. But I wasn't ready to admit it to Cary. I wasn't about to give him the satisfaction. I had tried to apologize to him time after time, and he hadn't accepted.

I stared at him. "Are you finished?" I asked.

He looked surprised. "Uh — yes, I guess so," he answered.

"Okay, then. Thanks for coming by." I turned my back on him and leaned over my desk, pretending to be absorbed in my work.

I heard him shift from foot to foot behind me. He cleared his throat once. Then he left the room.

As soon as I heard his footsteps on the stairs, I dropped the pose and slumped over my desk.

This was ridiculous. Cary and I had created a humongous mess, and I didn't know how to clean it up. I was mad at him, he was mad at me. We'd both done dumb things. And neither of us was ready to forgive.

I looked down at my "biography." It was nothing I'd ever hand in. It had just been a way of blowing off steam. But the fact was that I did have to write a biography of Cary. And I wanted it to be good, since Ted was the one who had given me the assignment in the first place. His opinion meant a lot to me.

I picked up my pen again.

CARY RETLIN : A BIOGRAPHY
Cary grew up in Oak Hill —

I threw the pen down and put my head in my hands. I didn't know what to write about Cary. I didn't know what to *think* about Cary.

I crumpled the pages I'd written and tossed them into the trash basket. Then I gathered up my notes and stuck them back into my notebook. "Later for you, Cary Retlin," I muttered as I shoved the notebook into my backpack.

I headed downstairs and found Nannie in the kitchen, starting to put together a beef stew.

"Hey, Ms. K," she said. "Who was that boy? Someone you're — *interested* in?" She grinned and waggled her eyebrows.

I rolled my eyes. "Please," I said.

"He seemed nice enough," Nannie went on. "Polite, well-spoken — "

"Could we just forget about him?" I asked impatiently.

Nannie backed off immediately. "Sure," she said. "Sorry." One thing about Nannie is that she always knows when to tease and when not to. "Want to help me chop some carrots?" she asked. She handed me a knife. "About this big." She showed me the carrot she'd already cut up.

I started chopping. "Nannie," I asked, "do we still have those Christmas lights in the shape of chili peppers? I was thinking I'd like to use them as part of my party decorations."

"Sure," she answered. "I think they're in the garage. I'll help you find them later. How's the rest of your planning coming?"

I told her about my ideas for music, food, and games, and she offered a few of her own. We talked and chopped, and soon I began to feel more relaxed than I had in days.

The phone rang just as Nannie was asking me how much garlic I thought she should add.

"At least three cloves," I advised, reaching for the phone. "Hello?"

"Kristy, it's me, Claud."

"Hey, what's up?" Claudia sounded excited.

"My mom just heard from a friend of hers who works in the school library," she said. "The administration made its decision."

I held my breath. Judging by Claudia's tone, it was good news. But I wanted to hear her say it. "And?" I asked.

"Ted has his job back!"

Chapter 15

"Wait, no! That goes over here!" I motioned to Mary Anne, who was carrying a platter full of mini-pizzas. I couldn't believe she was about to put it down on the coffee table. Wasn't it obvious that I'd cleared a space for it on the main food table? Only desserts were supposed to go on the coffee table. The night of my party had finally arrived, and I was just a teensy bit nervous.

Mary Anne whirled around and followed my directions, placing the pizzas between a plate of nachos and a bowl of dip.

"Where are you going with that?" I demanded as Stacey walked through the room with a big bottle of Coke.

"Uh, to the kitchen?" she said. "Is this a test or something?"

"Very funny," I said without a smile. "The party is starting in — " I checked my watch — "fifteen minutes. I want to have everything in place before the guests arrive."

"Why, is Prince William coming?" Claudia asked. She'd joined us in the dining room. She was carrying a gorgeous centerpiece she'd made out of glass Christmas tree balls tied together with ribbon.

"No, Prince William is not coming," I said. "But I want everything to be perfect."

"Kristy, you have to chill," said Stacey. "It's going to be a great party. Everybody is psyched for it."

"Especially since Ted has his job back," Claudia added. "Everybody will be in a great mood."

I knew they were right. But I was finding it hard to relax, I guess because this was the first party I'd thrown on my own. I *was* grateful that Claudia and Stacey seemed to have declared a truce in honor of the party. I'm lucky to have such loyal friends.

The doorbell rang then, and I gasped. "That can't be guests already!" I cried. What a disaster. I hadn't even put out the cheese balls.

"It's probably just Dawn," said Mary Anne. "She was still napping off her jet lag when I left the house, but she said she'd be here as soon as she could."

We were having a mini BSC reunion that night. Dawn and her younger brother, Jeff, had just arrived from California to spend the holidays with their mom and Mary Anne and Mary Anne's dad. Mallory was home from boarding school for Christmas break. Abby, Jessi, and Shannon would be coming by too.

Mary Anne ran to answer the door while I headed for the kitchen to round up the cheese balls. When I returned to the dining room, Dawn was there. She was in the middle of giving Claudia a big hug, but when she saw me her eyes lit up.

"Kristy!" she said. "The place looks *awesome*. The decorations are great. And you guys all look excellent," she added, gazing around at us.

I was glad to hear she liked the decorations. I was pretty proud of myself. The chili pepper lights were strung around the dining room, and red candles were burning on the table. I'd hung ropes of evergreen (Watson had helped me pick them up at the nursery) all through the house, and our gigantic Christmas tree, hung with our traditional trimmings and dripping with tinsel, stood proudly in the living room. Claudia's centerpiece brightened the dining room table, and some paper chains that Karen and

Andrew had made were draped in the hallways. I'd even put our red and green guest towels in the downstairs bathroom.

As for our outfits, I had to agree with Dawn that everybody looked great. I was wearing a holiday version of my usual "uniform": instead of jeans I wore dark green corduroys, and I'd topped them with a bright red turtleneck. Stacey was wearing a red woolen miniskirt topped with a little red woolen jacket (she looked like a very hip Mrs. Claus). Claudia had on red-and-white-striped stockings (the candy cane look) and a white dress with red polka dots. Miniature green Christmas tree earrings dangled from her ears. Mary Anne looked beautiful in a navy blue velvet dress. And Dawn was doing Christmas California-style, in a white denim miniskirt and green silk blouse.

I took a deep breath. Maybe I *was* ready, after all. The doorbell rang again, and this time my heart didn't jump. The cheese balls were in place. There wasn't anything else to do but enjoy the party.

Mal and Jessi arrived together, giggling and talking and clearly thrilled to be reunited. I knew they'd monopolize each other all night long, but that was fine with me. I could imagine how hard it must be for best friends to be apart as much as they were.

Abby showed up next, with Shannon. "We walked over together," Shannon explained. "Have you looked outside? It's starting to snow."

Perfect. I couldn't have asked for a better evening. Very atmospheric. I ran to turn on the outdoor lights so we could watch the snow drifting down in the backyard.

Before I knew it, the party was in full swing. The doorbell was ringing every five seconds. Watson and my mom were in the kitchen, whipping up a batch of eggnog. Karen, Andrew, David Michael, and Emily Michelle were the "coat squad": They were piling everyone's coats on the guest room bed and pounding up and down the stairs as they raced one another to answer the door and help the next arriving guest. Sam and Charlie cranked up the volume on the CD player. They'd volunteered to DJ the party and keep the mood happy and fun.

It was an excellent party — I think. It went by in such a blur that I can't even be sure. I know that everybody seemed to be having a great time. I know that a bunch of people were dancing in the living room, and that almost all the food and all but one bottle of soda disappeared. There was lots of talking and plenty of laughter, especially in the corner where kids were playing Pictionary. I know I talked to just about every one of my guests, though only one of the conversations really sticks in my head (more about that later). But for the most part, the evening was like a speeded-up movie. A few scenes do stand out. For instance, I'll never forget the moment when Ted arrived. The doorbell rang while I happened to be standing in the front hall, so I was the one to answer the door.

"Ho, ho, ho!" Santa was on my doorstep — a Santa wearing red corduroy pants, a red flannel shirt, and a red Polarfleece hat. Instead of a white beard, his was black, and the bulge in his stomach was obviously fake.

"Ted!" I cried. I opened the door wide and motioned him inside. I was incredibly happy to see him, and I knew everybody else would be too. Sure enough, his entrance into the dining room brought on cheers and applause.

Watching him circulate through the room, I thought how great it was that things had worked out the way they had. Mrs. Dow and her group had made a lot of noise, but we'd been organized and determined and unafraid to take a stand, and our side had won in the end. I'd learned a good lesson from that.

I saw Claudia and Jeremy talking with Ted. Then

he moved on, and the two of them continued chatting. Jeremy had arrived with a corsage for Stacey, and he was her date for the party — but I couldn't help noticing that he kept gravitating toward Claudia. He seemed to be enjoying himself more when he was talking to her than when he was dancing or making the rounds with Stacey.

Logan had arrived on his own, to my relief. Still, he and Mary Anne spent most of the evening in separate rooms. He'd be nibbling on nachos in the dining room, and she'd be talking in the living room. She'd walk into the dining room to find some soda, and Logan would head for the CD player to request a song from Sam and Charlie.

When I asked Mary Anne if she was having a good time, she said she was. But at one point, she walked into the dining room, where Logan and Emily Bernstein were having a lively conversation about the book he was reading for Ted's class. I saw her notice them and watched a shadow cross her face. For a second, she looked a little sick. Then she stood up straight, helped herself to a cheese ball, and went back toward the living room. I could tell it wasn't easy for her to see Logan with another girl, even if they weren't dating.

All evening I'd been wondering if Cary would

show up. After all, I'd invited him way back when, before this mess had taken over our lives. But eventually I stopped watching to see who'd arrived every time the doorbell rang. It looked as if he'd decided to stay away.

Then, as I was walking through the living room, offering a box of chocolates around, I spotted him in a corner talking to Alan Gray. He must have arrived when I wasn't looking.

I held out the box to him. "Chocolate?" I asked.

Alan took three pieces and shoved them into his mouth all at once. "Thggs," he said as he chewed.

He is so gross sometimes.

Cary helped himself to a piece. "Good party," he said.

"Thanks," I replied. "Did you guys have some of the eggnog my mom and Watson made?"

"Eggnog? Where? I love eggnog!" Alan took off for the dining room.

Which left Cary and me standing there alone.

I glanced at him. He met my eyes. And he didn't turn and walk away.

Maybe it was time for us to clear the air, once and for all.

"Cary," I began, putting the chocolates down on a nearby table. "You were right. Whether or not that was your journal, I was wrong to read it. I'm sorry. Really, I am."

He nodded. "I know," he said. "Apology accepted." He stuck out his hand, and I shook it.

A feeling of relief washed over me. Finally! Suddenly, I felt a little tongue-tied. Now that we'd "made up," what would we talk about?

Cary broke the silence. "I have to say, I've had a great time writing your biography," he said. "There's more to you than I would have guessed."

"Well, thanks — I think," I said. I'd enjoyed writing his too. I'd found that writing about what I *didn't* know about him told as much as writing what I did know.

"I just have one more question," he said.

"Shoot," I told him.

"Where did you get the name Louie for your dog?"

I laughed. "It just came to us," I said. "He was a Louie. If you'd ever met him, you'd know what I mean." I looked at Cary. "Can I ask you one more question?"

"Anything," he said, smiling.

There was one thing I was dying to know. And this was my chance to find out. I looked into his eyes and asked, "Why did you really leave Illinois?"

Cary grinned. "Oh, that's simple," he answered. "See, the aliens decided it was time for me to go. So they beamed me up — and beamed me down right here in Stoneybrook."

"Cary! Come on, really."

"Oh, you want the *truth*?" Now he was in full Cary mode: smirk, eyebrow, and all. "Well, the townspeople accused me of being a witch, so my family had to leave in the dead of night — "

I just stood there, shaking my head. I was incredibly glad to have my old archenemy back.

About the Author

ANN MATTHEWS MARTIN was born on August 12, 1955. She grew up in Princeton, NJ, with her parents and her younger sister, Jane.

Although Ann used to be a teacher and then an editor of children's books, she's now a full-time writer. She gets ideas for her books from many different places. Some are based on personal experiences. Others are based on childhood memories and feelings. Many are written about contemporary problems or events.

All of Ann's characters, even the members of the Baby-sitters Club, are made up. (So is Stoneybrook.) But many of her characters are based on real people. Sometimes Ann names her characters after people she knows; other times she chooses names she likes.

In addition to the Baby-sitters Club books, Ann Martin has written many other books for children. Her favorite is *Ten Kids, No Pets* because she loves big families and she loves animals. Her favorite BSC book is *Kristy's Big Day*. (Kristy is her favorite baby-sitter.)

Ann M. Martin now lives in New York with her cats, Gussie, Woody, and Willy, and her dog, Sadie. Her hobbies are reading, sewing, and needlework — especially making clothes for children.

Look for #6

STACEY AND THE BOYFRIEND TRAP!

After lunch, I left the lunchroom with boys on my mind.

Maybe it was something about the new year.

First I'd resolved to contact Ethan.

Then Toby had popped up out of nowhere. And now he wanted to kiss me!

Next, Pete and I wound up working on this party together.

Then Robert joined. Robert — who had barely wanted to participate in anything since the last time I saw him — suddenly decided this was the time to get involved.

Adding to that, Wes, my big crush, had returned.

Now Sam.

And I couldn't forget Jeremy.

It was too much!